She had never before understood the attraction between her half-sister and Alex. But now she saw that, far from being a chilly Chandler, Alex radiated concern and kindness.

And his unexpected tenderness made her want to…want to…kiss him.

She tore her mind away from the thought. Alex didn't care about *her*. He simply wanted this baby.

A criminal defence attorney for twenty years, **Sue Swift** always sensed a creative wellspring bubbling inside her but didn't find her niche until attending a writing class with master teacher Bud Gardner. Within a short time Sue realised her creative outlet was romance fiction. Since she began writing her first novel, in November 1996, she's sold two books and two short stories. Her hobbies are hiking, bodysurfing and Kenpo karate, in which she's earned a second-degree black belt. Sue and her real-life hero of a husband maintain homes in Northern California and Maui, Hawaii. You may write to Sue at PO Box 241, Citrus Heights, CA 95611-0241, USA.

HIS BABY,
HER HEART

BY
SUE SWIFT

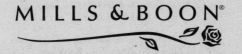

For my parents,
Sheila and Sheldon Swift,
two extraordinary people

*First published in Great Britain 2003
Harlequin Mills & Boon Limited,
Eton House, 18-24 Paradise Road, Richmond, Surrey TW9 1SR*

© Susan Freya Swift 2001

ISBN 0 263 83411 5

*Set in Times Roman 10½ on 12 pt.
02-1103-43368*

*Printed and bound in Spain
by Litografía Rosés, S.A., Barcelona*

Prologue

"I, Tamara Cohen Chandler, being of sound mind…"

Alex Chandler sat, numbed to the last ritual accompanying his wife's death. The presence of other family members in the wood-paneled law office receded to the back of his mind. He heard traffic outside the building bustling down Alhambra Boulevard, but the Sacramento rush hour seemed a thousand miles away.

"It is my dearest wish that my husband, Alexander Chandler, and my beloved half sister, Dena Cohen Randolph, cease the animosity between them."

To Alex's right, he could see Dena Randolph vainly brush at several dog hairs marring the sleeve of her black jacket. Alex tried to repress his disdain. Why couldn't the woman ever make herself presentable?

He'd tried to hide his dislike for his sister-in-law from Tamara. Evidently he'd failed.

"I request that Dena act as surrogate mother and carry to term one of my embryos, fertilized by Alexander Chandler."

"What?" Shock cracked Alex's leaden wall of grief.

Dena jerked upright, as though zapped with a live cattle prod. "As if I don't have enough problems already," she murmured.

Alex reluctantly sympathized. With four-year-old twins and their disappearing father, Dena's plate was full.

Her green eyes widened with bewilderment. "Did you know this was coming, Alex?"

He shook his head. "Tamara changed her will shortly after she was diagnosed. At the time, I didn't know what she did, and I didn't care. I was focused on her chemo, hoping she'd recover." Alex frowned. He'd worshiped his wife, but knew that sweet, well-meaning Tamara had also been manipulative and very, very smart. What on earth had she planned? Why?

"Well, I…I can't." Dena placed a hand on her stomach, as if caressing an imaginary pregnancy. "I know Tamara wanted a baby, but…I just can't bear a child and then walk away. Not even for Tami. Maybe you can find someone else, Alex."

He breathed deeply, striving for calmness in the face of sudden chaos. He'd do anything to make his wife's dreams a reality, however distasteful Dena Randolph might be. Why didn't she feel the same commitment to Tamara's memory?

"Further," the attorney continued, "I bequeath my one-half ownership of said embryos to Dena Randolph with the specific instruction that only Dena be implanted with them."

Dena went white, pale cheeks contrasting with her Titian-red hair. Alex couldn't blame her. He felt faint himself. What had Tamara done? She'd snared them both. Now he and Dena owned the precious embryos.

"For medical costs, Dena's support during the pregnancy, and for the support of the baby, I hereby provide the sum of three hundred thousand dollars, to be managed by Alexander Chandler."

Dena blinked. Then blinked again, trying to reconnect with reality. Interiors by Tamara, her sister's business, must have been lucrative. But Dena's world revolved around her kids, not money.

She'd opened her mouth to turn it down flat when the attorney said, "In addition, I hereby bequeath the sum of two hundred thousand dollars to be held by Dena for the benefit of Miriam and Jackson Randolph, my beloved niece and nephew."

Dena sagged in her chair. Tamara had known Dena would dig ditches with her teeth for her children, if necessary. But she wouldn't have to, not with this generous bequest. The funds would pay for cars and college, maybe even help buy them homes, luxuries her small landscaping business could never support.

Tamara had adored the kids, so no strings were attached to the trust. But Dena's conscience wouldn't let her rest if she didn't ponder her sister's last request. How could she repay such generosity with a refusal to grant Tami's dying wish?

Could she resist the money, which would provide so much for her sweet darlings?

Dena sucked in a deep breath, then peeked at Alex Chandler. With every blond hair in place, he sat rigidly, as if a poker had been shoved up his...

Yes, she could resist. Dena didn't want Alex, the android accountant, in her life. Eyeing him, she hesitated. "I won't have to sleep with you, will I?" She'd rather snuggle with a cyborg.

A glimmer of a smile twitched Alex's set lips. "I

don't think so. Our fertilized embryos are stored at her gynecologist's office. He defrosts them, implants a couple, and away we go.'' He gestured, exposing a perfectly starched French cuff secured by onyx links.

Dena dropped her head into her hands, digging her fingers through her hair. ''I can't believe it. What if one of us says no?''

''No baby, and Tamara loses her lifelong dream.''

''Oh, no,'' Dena moaned. Tears burned behind lids already swollen from crying. She fumbled for a tissue. ''Oh, Tami. Why me?''

Alex flicked imaginary lint from his immaculate, pin-striped sleeve. Not a shred of emotion showed on his too-handsome face. ''You're her half sister and, in her opinion, a great mother. She remarked often that she admired how easily you carried the twins.''

''That's true. It was pretty easy, considering everything.'' Considering that Dena had been dumped by her cheating ex-husband, for whom Lamaze was something a mouse ran through to get cheese. She winced. ''But another child? I have my hands full already.''

''It wouldn't be your child, Dena, but mine. Tamara trusted you to carry our baby to term and then give him up for me to raise.'' Alex's blue eyes gleamed, vivid and intense.

''I'm not a—a brood mare. I don't know if I can have a child and give it up.'' Dena couldn't keep a tremble out of her voice.

''You have to,'' Alex said. ''This was your sister's last wish. How can you say no?''

Chapter One

Six months later

On a chilly, bright March day, Alex sat in his attorney's office, waiting for Dena Randolph. She was late—as usual. If Tamara hadn't selected her half sister as their surrogate mother, Alex would have found someone more punctual.

Alex sipped stale coffee and tried to squelch his irritation. Had Dena shown up on time, the meeting would have concluded during his lunch hour. More than anything else, Alex wanted to go back to his office, bury himself in his work and forget how much he still missed Tamara.

Attorney Gary Kagan passed a sheaf of papers across his desk to Alex. "You can review the contract while we wait for Ms. Randolph."

Alex skimmed the closely typed pages. He'd wanted a contract so Dena would understand her place in the scheme of things. Dena, interfering and bossy, had off-beat ideas about child-rearing.

And her kids…Alex grimaced. He loved his niece and nephew, but the four-year-olds always seemed to be sticky, dirty, lost or in trouble. They were hardly poster children for Dena's parenting style.

Alex flipped through the pages. He saw everything he'd requested: the clauses stating what Dena had to do during the pregnancy, and what she couldn't do after the baby was born—namely, have unsupervised contact with his child or control over it. Gary had taken several months to draft what looked like a complex document.

"What happens if she doesn't sign it?" Alex asked.

Gary shrugged. "Both of you own the embryos, see? If she doesn't sign it, you don't cooperate. If you don't cooperate, no baby, and Tamara's dream dies right here."

Alex frowned. "That's rather blunt."

"That's life. Let me tell you—"

A loud pop interrupted Gary.

Alex's body involuntarily jerked. "Hey, are there gangbangers around here?" he asked his attorney.

"Only at night."

The chug of an overtaxed engine vibrated through the window. Alex cautiously scrambled over to the glass, then peeked through the pane.

Peering past a clipped hedge, he could see a battered yellow pickup, with fanciful vines and flowers painted on it in vivid rainbow colors. Dena's Gardens was stenciled in purple on the door. Dena's pickup backfired again as she reversed into a nearby parking space. Black smoke billowed from the muffler. Alex wondered if the pickup complied with California's strict antismog laws. Probably not, knowing Dena.

He raised his brows. "Guess who."

Gary joined Alex at the window. "She really ought to replace that old clunker pretty soon."

"She'd better. I won't have the mother of my child riding around in that piece of junk. It looks dangerous."

The door of the truck squealed as Dena opened it. Hinges need oil or something, Alex thought. He kept some in the trunk of his car. He'd take care of that squeak before she left.

Alex watched Dena climb down from the cab of the truck. Her faded jeans had dirt ground into the knees. She wore heavy work boots. He winced.

Dena strode toward the building that housed the office of Alex's attorney. The grind and clatter of her work boots on the pavement echoed her tripping heart.

She'd have this baby for her sister's sake, but she wanted to avoid involvement with Alex Chandler. Unfortunately, the two goals were incompatible, thrusting her into a messy situation for at least nine months. More, actually, since after the baby's birth, she couldn't evade responsibility for the child and didn't plan to try. She'd become an auntie, and in her mind, that implied a bond of love and trust that would tie everyone together...including Alex.

Dena sighed inwardly and wondered, for the umpteenth time, why her clever, talented sister had married Alex. Sure, he was good-looking, if you liked the icy, Nordic type. But Tamara, who'd been more beautiful than any Miss America, could have chosen anyone in the world for her mate.

Why Alex, the chilly Chandler? Lately he'd become even more remote, responding to phone calls curtly, if at all. Certain that he suffered over Tamara's passing, Dena hadn't pushed him out of his protective shell.

Dena yanked open the glass door of the brick-fronted building a little too hard. It whacked against a wall, but she ignored the bang in favor of her roiling thoughts.

What kind of a parent would Alex be? Unnerved, Dena stopped short in the middle of the carpeted lobby. She didn't want her baby niece or nephew growing up into a Popsicle person like Alex.

She better make sure this kid had all the love every child deserved.

Dena straightened her shoulders, firmed her resolve and marched into Gary Kagan's office. She forced a smile onto her face to disguise the determination in her heart.

When Dena entered, Alex, already irritated due to her lateness, couldn't behave cordially to her no matter how hard he tried. Her messy red mop, carelessly pinned at the top of her head in a knot, had started to fall down. Tendrils of her hair framed her face in a manner Alex knew some men might find sexy, sensual. But not Alex. Dena Randolph wasn't his type. She'd never be his type. Ever.

"Alex, Mr. Kagan," she greeted them, sounding a little breathless.

"Gary, please." His attorney puffed out his thin chest.

She gave him a dazzling, Rita Hayworth smile. "Gary."

Was it Alex's imagination, or did she add a sultry slur to the name? He hoped not. The mother of his child would have no business running around with other men. Alex expected Dena to live a quiet, safe life while she carried his baby.

He cleared his throat. "Good afternoon, Dena."

"Hiya." She plopped into a plush green chair in front of Gary's desk and picked up the contract. "So, is this the dastardly document?"

Gary laughed, and Dena winked at him. Alex didn't like her come-hither look. Hopefully his child wouldn't flirt. If the baby was a girl, he'd keep her at home until she was thirty.

"I hope you don't find it dastardly." Gary resumed his seat behind the desk.

"So it's an amiable agreement instead." She grinned.

"We think it's quite reasonable." Alex sat in a chair next to hers, then immediately regretted his action. She didn't smell like a person who'd labored that morning, but like a woman. A very sensual woman, with a fresh, flowery scent.

He sat back in his chair, hoping to escape her fragrant aura. He didn't want to enjoy Dena's aroma, her aura, or her anything. She was his wife's sister. Her half sister, but still…Dena? Attractive? No. Never.

Raising an eyebrow, she flipped through the pages. She didn't appear to read it at all. "Is this the usual kind of contract for this situation?"

"There really isn't a usual kind of contract for this. Surrogate motherhood isn't that common. There aren't many standard contracts. Believe me, I looked." Gary fiddled with a pen. "I drafted one from scratch."

"Termination of all parental rights," Dena read aloud. "What's that?"

"In essence, Alex will raise the child and be financially responsible for him or her." Gary nodded at Alex.

Alex tensed. The clause meant much more than that. If Dena signed, she'd be giving up the baby.

"That goes without saying." Dena sighed. "I'd love more kids, but I can't afford them."

Alex relaxed. "If this surrogacy is successful, perhaps you will be able to manage another child. Tamara left the twins a substantial sum of money."

Dena's lips tightened. "This has nothing to do with money. The baby was my sister's dying wish."

"So it was," Alex said in a smooth tone of voice. He wanted to soothe Dena's unsettled feelings.

"What's this? No unsupervised contact with the baby?" Dena glared at him, eyes glittering like shards of green glass. "Are you kidding? This is my flesh and blood we're talking about."

He exchanged a glance with Gary. Dena wasn't going to be a pushover.

Alex kept his voice calm. "How many aunts have unsupervised time with nieces and nephews?"

"Plenty. Tamara often took my kids to the zoo and to the park, remember? I wasn't there to *supervise*." Sarcasm sharpened her voice.

Alex sighed. Dena was right. Tamara had adored Jack and Miri. The twins had been a big part of her desire for children of her own.

"Besides, you'll want me to help with the baby."

Alex tried not to look superior. "I doubt that."

She lost the angry sparkle in her eyes. "So you think you know it all, huh, Alex?" She started to laugh.

"I'm sure I can raise my child without your assistance. You handle two, don't you? Why can't I take care of one?''

Her giggles continuing, she groped in her pocket and pulled out a tissue. ''Oh, no problem. You'll have no problem at all. I'm sure you can raise this kid all by yourself. After all, you did so well with the twins.'' She dabbed at the tears of laughter leaking from the corners of her eyes, visibly trying to control her mirth.

Alex felt himself reddening.

Gary looked interested. ''What about the twins?''

''One time when Alex and Tamara took my son and daughter to Land Park, Tamara took Miriam to Fairy Tale Town and Alex had responsibility for Jack. When Alex wasn't paying attention—''

''He sneaked out of the men's room. I was... indisposed. And it was just for a few seconds! It could have happened to anyone.''

Dena grinned. ''Jack found his way to the Land Park zoo and tried to climb onto the chimps' cage. All the zookeepers said he was very charming. Apparently he entertained a large crowd of people, giving the chimps screeching lessons.''

Alex glowered. ''My child won't be like that.'' *Especially if I keep you away.*

''Of course not.'' Dena's tone was patronizing. ''Your baby will be a perfect paragon of all the virtues under your wise guidance.''

Gary laughed. Alex glared at his attorney, who was supposed to be on *his* side.

''And what about breast-feeding?'' Dena asked.

''Breast-feeding?'' Alex had never in his life given any thought to the subject. Breast-feeding. He stared at Dena's chest. He envisioned his baby sucking from one of her breasts, which were now snugly clad in a worn yellow T-shirt with the purple Dena's Gardens logo on the front.

He'd never checked out Dena's breasts, but they were high, round breasts, perky and, well, touchable. They'd fit nicely in his hands.

He didn't want this fantasy. Adjusting his trousers, he pushed the image away, quick. Hot, he inserted a finger into his too-tight collar and tugged it away from his throat.

"I won't breast-feed with an audience." Dena folded her arms across her chest. "Makes me nervous. If I'm nervous, it affects the flow. You want your baby to breast-feed, right? That's very important."

"She's right. Breast-feeding is very important." Gary gawked at Dena, hunger clear in his eyes.

Alex drew in a breath, then let it out slowly, trying to slow his galloping pulse. "Okay, you're right. Cross it out."

"Thank you." With an air of triumph, Dena plucked the pen from Gary's fingers and scribbled out the offending clause. She dropped the pen back onto the desk.

Struggling to ignore Alex's disturbing presence, Dena lowered her gaze to the contract. From the first day they'd met, he'd ruffled her nerves, with his disapproving attitude and disparaging comments. She resolved not to let him get to her.

But that would be hard, very hard. Alex was a handsome man, if a little cold. But his recent experiences had cracked his corporate-clone shell, letting an appealing vulnerability show through. His blue eyes held a new maturity—

Cut this out, Dena! He's not for you!

Alex waited, anxious, as Dena continued to read. She rested her chin on her palm. The light caught her cheekbone, emphasizing its elegant curve. *So like Tamara's.* He gulped.

Tamara had been a slight sylph of a woman, a petite blonde with dainty features and hair like moonbeams. Tall, voluptuous Dena had always struck Alex as a larger, rougher version of his refined wife.

Now he found himself seeing Dena in a new way. The shape of her face. The tilt of her shimmering green eyes. In fact—

"Alex, this is very interesting." Dena raised a confused gaze from the contract. "You want to be my Lamaze partner?"

"Of course. Who else?"

"Mom went with me for the twins."

"Where was Steve?" Alex asked before he remembered Dena's husband had left her when he discovered she was pregnant with twins. Alex would rather have bitten off his tongue than remind Dena of that dark period in her life. "I'm sorry."

"It's okay. I'm over it." She shot him a breezy, careless smile. "I'm just surprised at you, that's all."

"Don't be. Dena, this baby means a lot to me. I'll be by your side every moment. You won't have to worry about anything."

"A supportive man. What a novel concept." She picked up the pen and signed at the bottom of the last page. "Okay, we're done. I'm gonna go eat. I have a short lunch break before I have to get to another job."

"We would have been finished sooner if you'd arrived on time," Alex said. "And you would have had enough time to read the whole contract."

"I've read enough." She stood, turned to the door and zipped out.

Alex looked at Gary, whose mouth was open.

The attorney closed his lips with an audible snap. "What came over her?"

"I don't know, but I'm going to find out." Alex left the office to follow Dena, who was halfway to her truck. He couldn't help noticing the way her worn jeans clasped her fit, firm bottom. *Stop it, Alex!*

He shoved her derriere out of his thoughts before he caught up with her in the parking lot. "What's going on? I thought you were going to work over that contract with a fine-toothed comb."

"So did I." Dena unlocked the door of her truck.

"Wait right there." Alex trotted to his car, opened the trunk and removed his tool kit. Finding some solvent in a spray can, he returned to Dena, who now sat inside her pickup.

"Turn your head." Alex sprayed the hinges. He wanted the mother of his child in perfect health before the embryo was implanted, so he used his free hand as a screen to keep the vapor away from Dena's nostrils.

He accidentally touched her cheek with his palm. Startled, he jerked away. "Sorry," he mumbled, shaken. Though she worked outside, her skin wasn't roughened by the sky and wind. Instead, she felt satin smooth, petal soft.

Again, he inhaled her scent. He ignored it.

Dena lurched back into the seat, her full lips pale and set. "Did I get some in your eyes? I tried not to." He capped the oil container.

"It's okay." But she still looked teary.

"So why did you sign the contract?"

Dena squirmed in her seat. "B-because I trust you."

He stared at her for several seconds before he remembered to smile. Dena Randolph had complimented him. Must be a historic occasion. As far as he knew, she'd never said anything nice about him. He was aware she called him Android Accountant Alex, the Corporate Clone. "Are you feeling all right?"

She gave a shaky laugh. "Not really. I'm hungry. I need to eat before my next job, and you probably want to go back to work."

"Yeah, well, yeah." He was completely tongue-tied. Alex hadn't known that contact with Dena Randolph could cause loss of his voice and his sanity.

As she drove away, he stood in the parking lot watching the retreating tailgate of her truck. He remained motionless long after it had disappeared from view.

He didn't understand. He didn't understand either her bitterness or her surprise at his conduct. *A supportive man. What a novel concept.* Her sour attitude didn't make sense. Tamara had described a happy childhood. Neither of his mother-in-law's husbands had left, they'd died. Dena hadn't come from a broken home.

If she'd truly gotten over Steve's desertion, why the cynicism?

Scratch a cynic and there's an idealist whose heart's been broken. Where had Alex heard that before?

Today, Dena had revealed depths he hadn't known existed. What strange new relationship would he and Dena forge?

Alex shook his head to clear his mind of all stray thoughts. None of this mattered. Only the baby mattered, but he knew that Dena's emotions would affect his unborn child's development.

His task was clear. He'd protect Dena and keep her happy, despite his mixed feelings about the woman.

And she was absolutely not going to get to him. Alex sucked in a deep breath, remembering the sweep of Dena's red hair over her flushed cheeks, her voluptuous breasts pressing against her T-shirt, and her backside in those tight, faded jeans. He couldn't repress his groan.

He had lustful thoughts about his dead wife's sister. What was wrong with him?

Clutching the steering wheel, Dena turned out of the parking lot and onto Alhambra Boulevard. He'd gotten to her. Android Alex had managed to slip under her skin and make her cry.

Like a chigger.

Dena remembered Steve's reaction when they'd learned she was pregnant. He'd been…startled, then accepting. But he'd chafed under the changes she made in their lives. She socialized less and slept more. She quit making caffeinated coffee in the mornings and didn't serve wine or beer. She'd asked him to smoke his cigarettes outside.

He'd rebelled against the idea of assisting her with the birth, chuckling that he never could stand the sight of blood. So going with her to Lamaze was out.

When he'd seen on the ultrasound screen two hearts beating in her womb, he'd fallen silent. She'd been excited and assumed that his reaction meant that he was too stunned with joy to speak.

Less than a month later, her husband—the man with whom she'd made a lifelong commitment—was gone, after cheating on her with every willing woman in the neighborhood. A geologist, Steve had dumped his boring government job to chase his dreams of wealth in the Saudi Arabian oil fields.

He'd discarded his family the way a snake sheds its skin. He hadn't contested the divorce. Occasionally he sent support checks. He wrote or phoned the twins even more rarely.

Steve Randolph had never met his children.

Dena stopped at a light and rested her forehead on the steering wheel. Waves of anger swept through her, leaving her shaky. Try as she might, she couldn't suppress the rage that always engulfed her when she thought about Steve. *This doesn't help,* she told herself. She'd never move forward with her life if she couldn't find peace in her own soul with Steve and his betrayals.

She threw Steve out of her mind. He was the past. He didn't matter anymore.

When the light changed to green, Dena accelerated through the intersection.

And now Alex Chandler wanted to be her Lamaze partner. Deeply touched by the promise he made to stay by her side when the baby came, she felt she had to sign the contract.

But now she had regrets. Had she acted too hastily?

She supposed she should be grateful for his caring attitude, but she didn't trust him, and the habit of independence from men had become deeply ingrained.

If Alex was going to be her Lamaze coach, that meant he'd be present when she gave birth. That he wanted to be there hadn't occurred to her. She didn't want such intimacy with Alex Chandler. She didn't like it. It made her feel...invaded, intruded upon.

On the other hand, she'd agreed to bear his child. Few acts were more intimate. But the surrogacy made a mockery of intimacy, didn't it? The baby would be Tamara's, not hers.

Dena shook her head. She didn't want to get close to Alex in any way. He was her sister's husband. Intimacy would seem just plain weird.

She remembered the touch of his hand on her cheek, which had been the first time a man had touched her for years. The gentle stroke had felt warm and tingly. Good. Too good.

She reminded herself that the caress had been accidental, and his concern for her based on the fact that she'd be the vessel for his child.

They'd never liked each other and probably never would.

Chapter Two

In some strange way, driving Tamara's sleek, silver Jag made Alex feel closer to her. Yet even this fuzzy-warm nostalgia for Tami couldn't mask his nervousness at the thought of seeing Dena again. He fingered the bundle of papers on the leather seat as he turned onto Fair Oaks Boulevard, fighting rush-hour traffic all the way.

Dena hadn't taken a copy of the surrogacy contract with her when she abruptly left Gary's office. Although a secretary could have mailed it, Alex liked having an excuse to drop by. He needed to visit Dena. He wanted to keep tabs on the woman who would carry his child.

Why had Tamara selected her half sister? Alex tapped the steering wheel with exasperated fingers. Would matters be easier with a stranger? Perhaps, but Dena was an honest person who wouldn't break her word. She'd give up the baby to him when the time came, so Alex could devote himself to his and Tamara's child.

He made a right turn onto Shadownook. At the end of the tree-lined cul-de-sac stood the old house that the

Randolphs had bought when they discovered Dena's pregnancy. Set back from the shallow curb, the rambling two-story home looked as though it had been designed for a houseful of kids. The open garage held her old clunker of a truck. Nearby, gardening tools hung on the wall in neat rows.

When Alex parked at the end of the driveway, he could see the twins' tree house nestled on a low branch of one of the huge old oaks rimming the property. Raised-bed gardens, clothed in new spring leaves, dotted the wide lawn. Kneeling, Dena dug in one, intent upon some unknown task.

He could see Jack and Miri playing on the lawn with Dena's golden retriever. Smiles lit the twins' grubby faces. Their dark hair stood up in spikes; the knees of their pants were torn and dirty.

Alex opened the Jag's door. Now he could hear the kids at play. The twins' raucous shouts changed to squeals of delight.

"Unka Alex! Unka Alex!" Oblivious to his charcoal-gray three-piece suit, Miri hugged him around the knees. She left smears of mud on his slacks.

Alex repressed a wince, knowing that the suit could be cleaned, but a child's broken heart might never mend. He picked up the little girl, allowing her to give him a big kiss, sticky with some mysterious snack she'd eaten. All the Cohens—even the Cohen-Randolph kids—were very touchy-feely, unlike the Chandlers. Alex hoped to achieve a happy medium with his child.

"Uncle Alex!" Jack hollered, his little legs pumping as he raced toward Alex. "Mom! Uncle Alex is here!"

Alex walked toward Dena, still carrying Miri. Jack trailed behind.

"Hello, Dena."

She looked up. Knee-deep in the loamy bed, which was half-planted with strawberry seedlings, Dena epitomized the perfect gardener. Wearing a battered straw hat, knee pads strapped around her coveralls, and sturdy gloves to protect her hands, Dena was dressed to kill… weeds.

She swiped a stray red hair off her face, leaving a streak of dirt on one high cheekbone. "Hi, Alex."

"Mommy, can Unka Alex stay for dinner?" Miri asked. "You said we have to love him more now that Auntie Tami's gone."

Smiling, Dena met Alex's clear blue gaze. "Of course Uncle Alex can have dinner with us, if he wants."

Alex felt his neck flush. So they'd discussed him. Not surprising. The Cohens were chatty as well as touchy-feely. Embarrassed but pleased, he said, "I'd like to stay if it doesn't inconvenience you. There are a few things I want to go over later."

"Yay! Uncle Alex, Uncle Alex!" Jack tried to climb up Alex to join Miri.

"Jack, don't grab at Uncle Alex's belt. He'll pick you up when he's ready."

Miriam smirked.

"Miri, stop that. Both of you, go play catch with the dog. Goldie!" Dena's high, sharp whistle sliced through Alex's eardrums.

Dena's golden retriever trotted up, two tennis balls clutched in her jaw. Goldie's tail waved and she rubbed against Alex, leaving a load of her blond hairs on his pants. She looked at his face with adoring brown eyes.

Alex put down Miriam. "Miri, get a ball from Goldie and go play." He didn't want dog spit all over his hands.

The twins scampered away with the dog. "Alex, could you keep an eye on them?" Dena asked. "After I get the rest of the strawberry sets planted, I need to shower and make dinner.''

"Oh, sure.''

"If you want to stay out of the firing line, you can sit on the porch.'' Dena nodded at the screened veranda circling her weathered, redwood home.

While the kids romped with Goldie, Alex took his briefcase and the contract from the Jag, then retreated to the enclosed porch. He settled himself on a rattan couch upholstered in a flower print. Dividing his attention between Dena and the twins, he flipped through the *Wall Street Journal.*

Dena soon finished and went into the house. She emerged a few minutes later with two beers in hand. She plopped down next to Alex on the couch, offering him a bottle.

"When can you go to the doctor's office for the implant procedure?'' Alex gave her the copy of the surrogacy contract she'd left in Gary's office.

She dropped it onto the couch between them. A symbol of their divisions, he thought.

But she sat close enough to touch. "When do you want this baby born?''

He caught her scent, something flowery. To cover his unease at her nearness, he took a swig of his beer. "I never thought about it. Does it make a difference?''

"It may be an old wives' tale, but a lot of people think that children born in the spring and summer have a better chance at life.'' Dena twisted off the cap from her bottle.

"In what ways?''

"Higher birth weight, lower infant mortality, that sort of thing.'' She sipped her beer.

Alex winced at the thought of infant mortality. How

could Dena sound so casual? "But we'd have to wait until August to have a baby born in May. That's five months away." Besides, he didn't want to base anything about his baby on rumors or myths. He preferred research. "I think we should start right away. The first implant might not take."

"You mean I might have to do this procedure more than once?" Dena set her bottle onto the floor next to her feet.

Alex faltered. "I'm afraid so. Remember what happened with Tamara? We could never get an embryo to stay."

Dena's soft, full lips tightened. "I'm sorry you and Tamara had to go through that. We can start whenever you're ready. Just give me enough notice so I can reschedule my jobs and find child care for the twins."

"Can Irina watch the twins? I'd volunteer, but I'd like to be nearby."

"Hmm. If you want Mom to baby-sit you have to check with her. Obviously she's my first choice, but we have to work around her catering jobs and her production schedule. The director won't allow the twins on the set."

Dena's mother, caterer Irina Cohen, starred in a cable television show, *Irina Cooks!* It had made Ashkenazi Jewish cuisine wildly popular in the Sacramento area. "Why not?" Alex asked.

"You didn't hear? Oh, this happened when you took Tamara to that cancer place back east."

"Sloan-Kettering." The treatments there had left Tami sick and bald. Alex swallowed down the painful memories with a gulp of brew.

"Yeah. Mom took the kids to the set one day, sure everyone would love her adorable grandchildren."

"They really are cute." *Messy, but cute.* Alex watched Jack tease Goldie with a tennis ball. Far from seeming offended, the retriever wagged her tail and barked, jumping up and down. She chased Jack around the side of the house.

"Anyway, Miri got into the food. She was in her meal-wearing phase, when everything went into her hair or on her chest."

"She must have been quite a sight." Alex knew that his child would never do any such thing.

Dena continued, "You know how much Jack likes to climb? He got onto one of the gaffer's booms." Picking up her bottle, she stood and stretched. The movement lifted her breasts inside her snug T-shirt. "Well, I'm gonna hit the shower. See ya in a while."

The door slammed behind her as she went into the house.

Alex picked up the newspaper, but the discussion of mutual fund investments in high-tech security systems couldn't hold his interest.

Unwittingly, his thoughts strayed to Dena. He imagined her ascending the stairs, entering her bedroom and stripping off her dirty clothes, exposing her strong body and round breasts. They'd rise higher when she unclipped her long, wavy hair.

He yanked his mind back to a columnist's analysis of the Fed's recent change in interest rates. This train of thought was disrespectful to Tamara. Besides, he didn't find Dena attractive. Did he?

She'd switch on the shower and step in, wiggling her toes with pleasure at the splash of the warm water. When she shampooed, the water would slick her hair into dark, wild whips. Foam would cascade down her curvy form, clinging to her nipples. Without inhibition, she'd toss her head when she rinsed.

Was Dena's libido as fiery as her mane?

What was he thinking? His X-rated fantasies starring Dena shocked him. He hadn't found anyone sexy for well over a year—hadn't had an erotic impulse since Tamara had started chemo and grown so sick. He'd devoted himself to her healing. Then, when it became clear she wasn't going to make it, he'd helped to ease her way out of this world into a better place.

His body's yearning spun him into tumult. He hadn't wanted to make love for months. And now, it was Dena Randolph who had prodded his dormant libido into life.

Dena, of all people. She didn't turn him on, he silently argued to himself. It was just that he'd been without a woman for so very long. She happened to be nearby when the natural reawakening of his sexual urges took place.

His soul cried out for Tamara. In a way, he felt he was losing her again. Another little bit of his life with her had receded into the past.

He desperately wanted to make love again, but he could never have the woman he needed: his wife. With a sickening lurch in his stomach, he accepted that he'd never again touch her, never hold her, never bury himself deep inside her.

Never love her.

He blinked back tears. Dear God, how he missed Tami. He took out a handkerchief and rubbed his face.

Closing his eyes, he recalled one of their last conversations. She'd framed his face in her hands and, looking at him with those lovely blue eyes, said, "Alex, listen to me. After I'm gone, I want you to go on."

He'd argued with her, telling her that she'd soon be well and they'd be happy together again.

She'd shaken her head. "No. Please don't belittle me by hiding the facts. I know I'm dying. Promise me something."

"Anything."

"Promise me you'll go on. Promise me you'll have a good life, Alex. Promise me you'll find someone to love."

Now he leaned back and sighed. "I'm trying, Tami," he said aloud. "But it's so damn hard—"

A wet nose thrust into his palm, making his body jerk and his thoughts scatter. Goldie again nudged his hand, inviting him to play. Alex blinked, returning to the present.

He looked across the lawn for the twins, but Dena's yard, dim and quiet in the waning light, held no chattering, screeching children.

Where were the twins? Jumping to his feet, Alex scanned the front yard. Guilt flooded him. How could he have been so inattentive?

He groaned. If he couldn't watch two four-year-olds, how could he raise a baby alone? How did Dena do it? His respect for her soared.

His shoes clattering down the three wooden steps to the lawn, Alex left the veranda when he realized that he couldn't see anything. He strode to the rear of the house. The backyard had an eastern exposure and didn't catch any of the western sun.

"Jack! Miri!" he called.

Alex could hear the low murmur of a fountain, part

of a water feature Dena had installed last summer. He walked over to make sure that neither of the kids had gone swimming. His mind refused to entertain the possibility that one had drowned.

Water chuckled over the rocks lining the pond Dena had created. A turtle raised its head, then ducked as Goldie approached. The retriever nudged Alex's hand, then dropped a wet ball into it.

"Yuck!" Alex restrained himself from wiping his palm on his gabardine trousers. Holding the ball with only his fingertips, he tossed it for the dog.

Goldie chased it to the front of the house. Alex followed. On the way, he checked the foliage for twins.

Nothing.

He broke into a sweat despite the cool evening air. Where could they be? He checked the trees. Though Jack enjoyed climbing, they were clear. Then he spotted the twins' tree house, a makeshift shack that a previous homeowner must have built years before the Randolphs moved in. He could see someone had improved it—Dena?—because fresh slats secured it to the big old valley oak in which it was anchored. The rope ladder that dropped from it to the lawn looked new.

Alex eyed the ladder, then his wing tips. He frowned. He didn't want to climb up to the tree house. Although Dena had fortified it, he didn't know if the flimsy structure could bear an adult's weight.

"Jack? Miri!"

Silence.

But the little scamps could be hiding. He'd bet money that, on some days, their favorite sport was eluding Uncle Alex.

With a resigned sigh, Alex set his right foot into one

of the lower rungs of the ladder, then skipped two as he climbed. After a few steps, he could peek into the twins' lair.

Empty.

He turned to descend as a voice came from the screened porch. "Alex?"

His foot slipped.

"Alex, what on earth—"

His other foot tangled in the ropes, and he fell to the soft, cold grass at the bottom of the tree. Embarrassed but unhurt, he took a moment to mourn his charcoal-gray suit. He feared it had taken too much abuse to survive. No doubt it was a goner.

He raised his head. Light from inside the house streamed through the stained glass inserts in the front door, illuminating the March evening.

Dena, freshly bathed and clad in a pink chenille bathrobe, stood on the porch. He could see her wet hair in a twist at the crown of her head, with a damp curl sticking to her cheek.

The twins, in a similar clean condition, stared at him. Dena carried Miri, who wore a red robe. Jack, clad in green sweats, had climbed onto a table, presumably to get a better view of Uncle Alex making a fool of himself.

He didn't want to admit that he'd been searching high and low for the twins. They'd obviously gone inside for their baths while he'd been lost in an erotic fantasy about their mother.

Goldie ambled over to Alex, stuck her nose into his face and chuffed in a friendly way. He caught the odor of kibble. She licked him.

Alex knelt, then stood. The seat and knees of his trousers felt damp. Probably grass-stained, as well. The elbows of his jacket were trashed. The dog had left golden hairs and saliva on his clothing.

Dena's home, glowing in the night, beckoned him to its warmth.

Chapter Three

Alex looked disheveled, a state in which Dena had never seen him at any time during his marriage to Tamara.

"Alex, use the little bathroom here to clean up. Dinner's in five, okay?" Dena held the front door open for him. "Kids, help me set the table."

If I cared about Alex, I'd be really worried about him, Dena thought as she led the twins and the dog to the kitchen. Despite herself, her heart went out to the poor guy. *He's devastated by losing Tamara.* Dena knew a dose of the twins would lift his spirits. Jack and Miri could test the patience of several saints, but they were sweet children who adored Alex.

Dena had worked hard to make her kitchen a cozy, homey place. A white-tiled counter separated the work space from the breakfast nook, where her family ate most meals at a big, wood farmhouse table. The twins' artwork decorated her refrigerator. Her daughter seemed to prefer flowers, butterflies and turtles, while Jack consistently drew houses with three-person families outside the front door. He even tried to include Goldie, though without much success.

Miri went to the low, whitewashed cupboard that housed the silverware and plates. "One, two, three." She counted blue-and-white gingham place mats. "Four, 'cuz Unka Alex is here, huh?" She put them on the table.

"That's right, darling." Dena turned to the refrigerator. She removed salad makings and put them on the wooden counter next to a bowl.

As Jack clattered flatware onto the table, Alex emerged from the hall. He'd washed and taken off his jacket, loosened his tie. He'd even rolled up his starched shirtsleeves, baring tanned, brawny forearms sprinkled with tiny blond hairs. They caught the light, glittering gold.

Dena's heartbeat quickened before she looked away, reminding herself that she had no business noticing Alex's arms. She had a legal contract with the husband of her deceased half sister. Period.

Alex sniffed. "Something smells good. Chicken?"

"Yeah." Dena opened the lid of her Crock-Pot, releasing a steamy, aromatic cloud. She poked the contents with a knife to make sure the fowl had cooked through.

He hovered behind her, too darn close. She scented a faint whiff of his aftershave, a fresh lime fragrance, tinctured by the grass that probably still clung to his pants. His nearness was simultaneously seductive and irritating. She didn't enjoy being crowded, but ignored her discomfort.

Peeking over her shoulder, he said, "How long did that cook?" His breath puffed on her neck.

The little hairs at her nape prickled and lifted. With a

nervous gulp, she managed to focus on his question. "I started it before I left this morning. You just put everything in and it cooks all day. It's really easy. Do you have a Crock-Pot, Alex?" She replaced the lid.

He shook his head. "Before I met Tamara, I was the fast-food king. She cooked, but made it clear I wasn't welcome in the kitchen."

Dena could understand that. "Your condo's kitchen is pretty small." He was making her crazy, his masculine presence somehow taking up all the room in her large work space.

"Can I do anything to help?"

She tried hard to overlook his engaging smile. *This is Alex, Dena. You don't like Alex, remember?* "Sure. Why don't you take care of the salad? All you need to do is rinse the vegetables and cut them into bite-size pieces."

"Dena, I'm not a complete moron." Chuckling, he leaned against the counter. "I can make a salad."

She grinned. "You said you were the fast-food king. I took you literally. When did you eat your last home-cooked meal?"

"At Irina's after the funeral." He tore apart a lettuce.

"That was more than six months ago, for heaven's sake. You're overdue. Alex, I'm sorry. We should have asked you over sooner, but—"

He stopped her with an upraised hand. "It's all right. The time just slipped away from us. Plus, I've been making an effort to stay busy."

Dena tried to suck air into her suddenly tight chest. "Oh, God, Alex, I still miss her so much." Shaky, she braced herself against the counter.

He moved in to hug her, and amazingly, his closeness wasn't oppressive, but just right. "Hey, none of that," he whispered into her ear. The small hairs at her temple shifted with his breath, tickling pleasantly. "If you start, then I'll start, and that can't be right for the kids."

She hugged him back, surprised by his warmth and affection. "I know." On the other hand, she didn't want to give her children the wrong impression of her relationship with their uncle Alex. After gently freeing herself, she walked to the table to supervise the twins, who'd watched, big-eyed.

"Miri, get the plates," Dena said, putting a casual note in her voice. "Jack, we're having soup tonight, so fetch me bowls, okay?" Returning to the kitchen, she unplugged the Crock-Pot and poured off the broth that had cooked with the chicken and vegetables.

Jack walked behind Alex, carrying four bowls to Dena.

"Good job, Jack." She stroked his dark, silky hair. "You did that with both hands. That was smart."

"What are you doing now?" Alex asked. The man was as curious as several cats. Opening a package of peeled baby carrots, he added half to the salad.

"Serving the soup. The twins like theirs lukewarm, though getting Miriam to eat it rather than bathe in it is always a chore." Dena scrutinized her daughter. Miriam now sat at her place at the table, hands folded, doing a "perfect child" imitation.

Dena knew better. Giving Miri a hard stare, Dena set bowls of soup at each place.

"Can I pretend that it's Japanese soup?" Jack asked. He stood on a chair to peer into his mother's face.

She looked into her son's round brown eyes, so like Steve's, but his open expression belonged only to Jack.

"I want you to try to use the spoon rather than pick up the bowl, okay?" Dena ruffled his hair, then checked the table, moving a couple of misplaced forks to their proper locations. "Sit down, please."

Alex chopped a tomato. "How soon is dinner? I'm ravenous."

"I bet, especially since you haven't had a decent meal for a long time. Did you also quit running?" Dena tried to check out the bod under Alex's fitted vest, shirt and trousers. He looked as though he was still in pretty good shape, despite his unhealthy diet. Wide shoulders tapering to slim hips and tight buns. Yum.

What was she thinking? She returned her attention on her children, where it belonged.

"Um, well, I've been concentrating on my work lately. I should probably start to jog again." He put the salad bowl on the table and sat in one of the empty chairs.

"That's Mommy's place," the twins chorused.

"Sit there." Miriam pointed an imperious finger.

Alex obeyed.

Dena drew in a breath. Unwittingly, Miriam had seated Alex at the head of the table, the spot Steve had occupied. Alex looked great in her husband's place, as though he belonged in it.

Dena swallowed. "Work. Right. Are you using work to, um, escape?"

He picked up his plate, examining it. "Kind of. You know, I like this Beatrix Potter china."

Dena noticed he'd quickly changed the subject.

"You gave it to us, Unka Alex. When we was three." Miri tapped her spoon against her plate.

"Were three," Alex said.

"Were three," Miriam repeated obediently. She must have liked the ringing noise, because she whacked harder.

Dena took the spoon away. "No."

Miri pushed out her lower lip.

"Miri, you'll get the spoon back if you eat your soup like a good girl."

The lip retracted. "Okay, Mommy."

Finding Miri unusually cooperative, Dena eyed her daughter with suspicion. Was her baby girl coming down with something? Dena felt Miri's forehead. She seemed fine. Maybe she was on her best behavior for Alex. If so, "Unka Alex" would be asked for dinner more often. Dena beamed at Alex.

Alex smiled back, unexpectedly cheered. Dinner proceeded without either twin swimming in the soup or even getting messy. Alex found himself both surprised and impressed by Dena's parenting skills. He'd been reading about the subject because he didn't want to repeat the mistakes of his mother and father. He could tell that Dena did many things right. Maybe it wasn't her fault that the twins occasionally acted up.

His thoughts strayed to Dena's ex. Steve, whom Alex had considered a nice guy, had shocked everyone when he disappeared into the Arabian desert. How could he have left his family? Alex looked around the table at three happy faces. He'd wanted this all his life.

Miriam stabbed a carrot with her fork and held it up to the light. "Carrot," she solemnly told her mother.

"That's right, Miri. Tell Uncle Alex about the carrots you grew, honey."

Miriam turned to him. "We grew carrots, Unka Alex. In preschool."

Alex said, "Were they nice carrots?"

"No." Miri shook her head in a decisive motion. "They was freaked."

"They were *forked*." Dena's girlish giggle blended with her daughter's. "Do you remember why?"

"Mommy said the ground had rocks. The carrots grew around the rocks. They went weird."

Jack thrust out his little chest. "My cokes was perfect."

"Your cokes?" Alex was mystified.

"*Cukes,*" Dena said. "Miriam, are you going to eat those carrots?"

Miriam, who'd been toying with her food, dropped her fork with a clatter and a guilty expression. "No," she said, sounding firm.

Alex wondered what Dena would do. Forbid dessert? Force Miriam to stay at the table until all her food was gone? He prepared to mentally take notes.

"Umm. Maybe I'll eat your carrots, then." Dena reached for Miriam's plate.

Miri frantically waved her hands. "*My* carrots!"

"Maybe Jack wants some more carrots." Dena looked at her son's dinner. "He's finished all of his."

"No no no no no!" Dragging her plate closer to her, Miriam enthusiastically crunched a carrot.

"Nice job, Dena." Alex swallowed a bite of the delicious chicken.

She winked at him, then put a finger to her lush lips in a hushing motion.

Was her sassy wink deliberately flirtatious?

No. It couldn't be. Alex decided he was dreaming.

"I'm done, Mommy." Jack took his plate over to the sink and carefully pushed it onto the counter, several inches higher than his head.

"Thank you, Jackson. You may go pick a book." Dena glanced at Miriam.

"I'm done, too. See?" Miriam pointed.

Using her fork, Dena flipped a lettuce leaf away from a corner of Miriam's plate. Beneath it hid a piece of chicken.

"Have you had enough to eat?"

"Uh-huh." Miriam batted green eyes, very like Dena's. She had Steve's dark hair combined with her mother's eyes and skin. One day, she'd break hearts. Did Dena break hearts? "I want to go now."

Alex saw a frown crease Dena's face. "Well, you had enough chicken and salad, and you drank your soup without making a mess. Okay, you can go. I'll be in soon to help you brush your teeth."

Miri left, and Alex asked, "Will they be all right wandering around unsupervised?"

Dena laughed. "They don't generally get into much trouble inside the house. This place is child-proofed, and their routine is to look at books quietly after supper." She adjusted the opening of her robe over the upper curves of her breasts.

The pink chenille robe warmly hugged her generous body. He bet Dena was a cozy, snuggly handful. He looked away. "Miriam didn't eat all her food." He hoped he didn't sound critical, especially since he and Dena seemed to be getting along so well…as long as he didn't ogle her. "Is that all right?"

"Yeah, it's okay. I probably gave her too much." She didn't appear to be offended. "They eat what they need. They're healthy. Eating lightly once or twice won't hurt them."

Alex picked up their now-empty plates and took them to the sink. "Can I wash up?" He figured that if he was a good guest, he'd be invited back. He wouldn't dwell on his earlier risqué fantasies. They were an aberration, nothing more.

"Oh, just stack them in the dishwasher. I'll turn it on later. Want to help me tuck them in?"

"Don't they have to brush their teeth?"

"First we brush teeth, then they're tucked in, then we read a book they choose. You take Jack, I'll do Miri." Dena left the kitchen.

"All right." Alex decided the experience would be good practice for later, when he raised his own baby. His heart bounced at the thought.

"Just remember to be firm. They'll play games and test you all night long if you let them."

Alex followed Dena to the living room. Jack, curled up with a picture book, sat on an overstuffed, plump couch, upholstered in dark red leather. For reasons known only to her, Miriam rolled around on the floor in front of the TV set. *Rugrats* occupied the TV screen.

So much for routines.

"Pick a book, Miri, it's time for bed." Dena tapped the toe of her bunny-shaped bedroom slipper on the gray carpet.

Miri stood and staggered around the room until she regained her footing. "I want *Cat in the Hat.*"

"I have it," Jack said.

Her little face crumpled. Tears threatened. "I want *Cat!*"

Here it comes, Alex thought. How would Dena rise to this challenge? He watched intently.

"Your copy is in your room. Come on, honey." Dena gave Miriam a little push. "We're going to brush our teeth in my bathroom. Jack, go with Alex." She flipped off the television.

Alex guided his nephew up the stairs, with Dena and Miriam behind him. He couldn't see Dena, but his awareness of her had increased exponentially. Her flowery, feminine scent filled his nostrils while the rustle of her robe engendered wild fantasies. What kind of nightgown did Dena wear under that cozy pink chenille? Did white lace or black satin cling to her curvy body?

Every one of Alex's muscles vibrated with a peculiarly sexual tension, new, different, and definitely unwanted.

After climbing the stairs, he followed Jack to the bathroom the twins shared. Out of the corner of his eye, Alex saw Dena and Miri head to a different room, presumably to use Dena's bathroom for Miriam's ablutions.

He relaxed. He feared these new feelings for Dena Randolph, and didn't want to experience them with her around.

Jack entered the bathroom and neatly placed his copy of *The Cat in the Hat* on the beige Formica counter. Plucking a green toothbrush from a holder shaped like Donald Duck, he held it under the water, then began to brush his teeth.

"Hold on there, buddy." Alex picked up the toothpaste. "You forgot something."

"Mommy said I don't have to use that." Jack looked up at Alex, his brown eyes wide and innocent.

Alex hesitated. Dena had some far-out ideas about child-rearing, and she'd been short of cash. Maybe Jack was telling the truth.

Dena buzzed in. "Jackson, have you brushed? Miri wants the sparkle toothpaste."

"He brushed, but he didn't use this yet." Alex brandished the tube.

"Oh, he's gotta have his fluoride." Dena applied paste to the green brush, then shot her son a pointed stare. "Don't try to scam Uncle Alex. Don't you want your teeth to be shiny and bright for the tooth fairy?"

Jack stared at the mirror. Leaning forward, he touched a finger to a front tooth and tried to wiggle it. ''Tooth fairy's never gonna come,'' he grumbled.

''The tooth fairy's going to come in about two years, Jack. Be ready.'' Dena dropped a kiss onto her son's dark head, then winked at Alex again before she bustled out.

Alex stood, silent and stunned, as Jack brushed, his mouth foamy with sparkle toothpaste.

Dena Randolph winked at me. Twice. An unexpected warmth started in the region of Alex's heart, then dropped like sand through a sieve, going straight to his libido.

Do *not* get turned on by Dena, he admonished himself.

Finishing, Jack rinsed his mouth, then tossed the brush into the sink. ''Can I watch more TV? Mom lets us stay up and watch TV after we brush.''

Alex rescued the brush and inserted it into the holder. ''Mom said book and bed. Now.'' *Fool me once, shame on you. Fool me twice, shame on me.*

The Cat in the Hat by Dr. Seuss in hand, he herded Jack to his room. Jack's bedroom, the ultimate little boy's hideout, was decorated in green-and-blue plaid. At the foot of his bed, a toy box overflowed with both twins' treasures: baseball gloves and Barbies, Nerf balls and Nintendo.

Jack climbed onto his bed, grabbing the stuffed teddy bear from his pillow to clutch it to his chest.

Alex pulled down the plaid comforter. ''Do you sleep in your sweats?''

''Nope.'' Jack tugged down his sweatpants, which stuck at his ankles. Alex helped, then dragged the sweatshirt over Jack's head. Underneath, Jack wore a white T-shirt and underpants.

Alex's heart swelled with love for this little being. He remembered when the twins had been born, tiny, red and squalling. Tamara had been over the moon and, openly envious of her sister, had started a campaign to have her own babies.

At the time, Alex didn't understand the attraction. But as the days passed, and the twins developed distinct, unique personalities, he understood. They were special children.

All of life's twists and turns had led Alex here, anxiously planning a foray into parenthood while putting his nephew to bed. Someday soon, Alex would be tucking in his own baby.

He took a deep breath. This was good. This was practice. "Want to read *Cat in the Hat?*" Alex waved the book in the air.

Jack settled back against his pillow. "Okay."

Alex read the children's tale, which followed the antics of a mischievous cat who turned the lives of a family topsy-turvy. He was irresistibly reminded of his wife, Tamara, whose will had turned everything upside down.

But he didn't regret anything. Not a single day, not a single moment. Every second with Tami had been a precious gift, all the more valued because she'd gone. He just wanted, one day, to recapture the wondrous magic of love. Could he be so lucky twice in one lifetime?

Dena peeked in. Her twinkling eyes filled him with nervous expectancy. What if she winked at him again?

She asked, "Is there a little boy in here who wants a good-night kiss?"

"Yes," Alex answered.

Jack glared. "*My* mommy." He reached for Dena.

Alex wanted to crawl under the bed.

Dena laughed easily. "That's what he meant, darling.'' Sitting across from Alex on Jack's bed, she took her son into her arms to embrace him.

A pang tore Alex's heart. His restrained, dignified mother had never held him with such open affection. He made a mental note to remind himself to give his child plenty of hugs and kisses. Maybe his baby wouldn't have a mother, but there'd be love to spare. *I'll make sure,* Alex told himself.

Lifting her head, Dena smiled brilliantly at him, warming him to his toes. ''Go in and kiss Miri goodnight. She's expecting you.''

Miriam's enclave was dim, lit only by a night-light in the shape of Mickey Mouse. Her sheets and other decor seemed to revolve around Mickey and Minnie's antics.

''Hey, sweetie.'' Alex advanced into the room to sit on the edge of her bed.

''Unka Alex.'' Miri, clad in a ruffled flannel nightgown, extended her arms for his embrace.

He leaned over, inhaling the scents of sparkle toothpaste and clean little girl. ''Sweet dreams, darling.''

''Nighty-night.'' Miri's arms dropped. Turning away from him, she cuddled her pillow, sighed once and appeared to fall instantly into sleep. Alex could see every muscle visibly easing into slumber.

Holding her hand, he watched Miri for a few minutes, struck by her total relaxation. She accepted him as an integral part of her world, he realized, and then wondered what responsibilities her love and acceptance engendered.

Dena came to the doorway and saw Alex, with an odd look on his face, disengage his hand from her daughter's.

Her spirit lifted. Though imperfect, her kids had a way of sneaking into people's hearts. She figured Alex still ached from the loss of Tami. Maybe the twins, with their open love for him, could help his battered soul.

Perhaps Alex wouldn't be the only one to benefit. Her little ones needed a father figure in their lives, and Alex could fill that role. Dena wanted to give them everything, but knew she fell woefully short in so many ways. She could be a lot of things to her children, but she couldn't be a father. As a beloved uncle, Alex could help.

Maybe this would work out. She didn't dare to think Alex could become something more for all of them.

But what if he left?

Dena started, a claw of fear slashing her guts. Steve, their own father, had left. Would the twins suffer if Alex remarried and left their lives?

Alex rose, then quietly walked to her. Taking her arm, he slipped out, closing the door after him.

Even through the robe, the warmth of his hand on her arm went straight to her heart. *Alex won't leave,* she knew with utter certainty.

But she'd thought the same about Steve, hadn't she?

Chapter Four

Dena descended the stairs with Alex behind her. He watched strands of her damp red hair escape its sloppy updo and tumble down her back in wisps. The pale skin at her nape looked tender, vulnerable.

Kissable.

When the phone rang, she gave an exasperated sigh. Her shoulders sagged. "Do me a very big favor, okay? Pour us both wine while I find a phone and deal with this. There's some Chardonnay open in the fridge."

"Find a phone?"

"The twins love the portable phones." The telephone rang again, this time from the vicinity of the couch. Dena began rooting beneath the sofa's cushions. As she bent over, he couldn't help checking out the swell of her derriere. "They think it's real fun to watch Mom run around searching when the phone rings. They're never where they belong—" She waved a handset triumphantly. "Hey, here we are. Hello?"

Alex stepped out of the room. When he came back, with two filled glasses in his hands, she still talked on the phone while curled into a corner of the couch. He sat at the other end.

"Blanche, you know I'll try like crazy to be there."

A pause ensued, during which Dena waved at Alex, flapping her fingers up and down, imitating a quacking duck. Blanche Desmond, his partner's fiancée, tended to chatter on and on. With a grin, he put a glass near Dena's hand. She took a sip while listening, then set the glass onto a burled coffee table in front of her. Alex tucked a coaster underneath it.

"No, I'm not insulted," Dena said. "Tamara was a good friend of yours and I understand that you'd want me to take her place in your wedding." She covered the receiver with her hand. "Alex, do you want to talk with Blanche?"

Alex shook his head and drew a finger across his throat in a cutting motion.

A smile twitched her lips. She ended the conversation, clicking off the phone before she turned to Alex. "You didn't want to talk with Greg's fiancée?"

"No. She always wants to commiserate about Tamara." He placed his left ankle onto the opposite knee. "Her pity's depressing. At least when I talk to you, it isn't about Tami all the time."

Dena's eyes widened. She curled her shapely legs under her, tucking her feet into the folds of her long robe. "But I think about her every day. I miss her a lot."

"I do, too, but I don't want to wallow for the rest of my life. Tami didn't want me to, but Blanche seems to think I should."

"You and I have a lot more to talk about than Tamara."

"Maybe she planned it that way." Alex grinned. "It would be just like her."

"Manipulative."

"Thoughtful," Alex corrected her.

Dena laughed. "Anyway, Blanche wants me to attend her wedding and take Tamara's place in the wedding party. By the time that comes around, I bet I'll look like a cow, but I didn't have the heart to refuse."

"I guess I'll escort you to Greg and Blanche's wedding." His mouth went dry, so he drank some wine. He'd never attended a formal event with Dena, who'd been married to Steve when Alex met her sister. Horror stories about Steve and Dena's nuptials had become family legend, so Alex and Tamara had eloped to Tahoe. They'd been certain that no wedding they could plan would satisfy the families, especially his picky, stuffy parents.

Dena Randolph at a formal wedding. He had a sudden vision of Dena in a bridesmaid's gown with gardening boots, or perhaps her bunny slippers. But that was foolish, wasn't it?

"Alex, we have to talk about the twins." Dena swirled the pale golden wine in her glass. "We should agree on this and stay consistent. How are we going to tell them? And what should we say?"

"About the baby? Hmm." Like the breast-feeding issue, Alex hadn't given the question any thought, and he hadn't a clue about how to proceed. "The implant might not take, so you wouldn't have to tell them anything at all."

Dena blanched. "I couldn't keep it from them. That

would be like lying. Alex, you can't lie to your kids. Besides, doesn't this involve several visits to the doctor? I have to tell them something, or they'll worry.''

''Yes, I've read that children are very insightful about such things.''

''The twins are very observant.'' Dena sipped the Chardonnay.

Alex grimaced. ''If one doesn't notice, the other one will.''

''Yeah. Maybe we should just tell them the truth.''

''That their mother is going to have Aunt Tami and Uncle Alex's baby?'' Putting down his glass with a clatter, he scratched his temple. ''How will they take that?''

Dena put her head in her hands. ''Lord knows. Maybe Mom is right. Maybe this whole business is crazy.''

Panic wrenched Alex's chest. He scooted closer to her, wondering if he should put his arm around her shoulders and hug her again, the way he had in the kitchen. He didn't know if she'd welcome his touch. Would another reassuring embrace be one too many? He took a cautious approach. ''Ah, er, Dena, are you having second thoughts?''

''Well, yes. What if it works? What if it doesn't work, and we go through all that trauma for nothing?'' She raised her head. Tears filmed her eyes. ''Have you thought about how you'd feel if I can't have this baby?''

Going limp, he let himself sink into the couch's soft cushions. The breath left his body with a *whoosh,* as though he'd taken a solid fist in the solar plexus. ''No, I haven't. Failure has never crossed my mind.''

''Alex, this baby was Tamara's dream. Why are you continuing it? I loved Tami. I did. But isn't this a bit…*much* in terms of faithfulness to one's departed spouse?''

''You don't understand.'' Alex couldn't help the frantic note in his voice. ''I want a family more than anything. The kind of family I never had. I'm not having this baby only to honor Tamara's memory, though that would be enough. I want this baby for…for me.''

Dena sat silently for a few moments, then said, ''There's something going on here I don't know about.''

He shrugged. ''There's no mystery. You know what my parents are like.''

''Mr. and Mrs. Frost, the chilly Chandlers.'' She clapped a hand over her mouth. ''Oh, I'm sorry!''

''That's what you call them? How appropriate.''

''I thought you'd be angry.'' Her voice was faint.

Alex looked at Dena sharply, squinting. Did her full lips quiver? ''Go on, laugh if you want.''

''I'm not laughing. It isn't funny. They really are as cold and repressed as they seem, huh?''

''Yes. I didn't realize it until I married Tamara and became a part of your family. I felt as though I'd walked out of a refrigerator and into the sunshine. That's why I want this baby, Dena. I need a family.''

''We're not enough for you?'' Dena couldn't keep the hurt out of her voice. *So much for Alex taking over here as Daddy.*

''Without Tamara, I'm not really a part of your family anymore.''

She winced. ''That's harsh.''

''That's the truth.''

''Alex, you're welcome over here anytime. Mom feels the same way.''

"Irina feels that I'm welcome in your home anytime?" Alex joked. "Nice of her."

Her lovely mouth pressed into a thin line. "You know what I mean."

"Yeah, I do. Dena, please don't go back on your word."

She sighed. "I won't. I just hope what we're doing is right, and everything comes out okay."

"I only care about your health and the baby's," Alex said with emphasis.

"Oh, don't worry about me. I'm healthy as a horse. My doctor told me I could have ten kids if I wanted them. If I can conceive using IVF, the baby will be fine." Dena stood.

Alex picked up the cue. It wasn't yet nine o'clock, but if she'd worked in people's yards all day, she must be tired. He rose, leaving his glass of wine on the table. He didn't want to drink it all when he was about to drive home.

"I'll show you to the door." Dena also left her glass as she turned toward the front of the house.

"Did we decide anything?" He followed her to the door, making a quick detour into the bathroom, where he'd left his jacket.

"Yes. We're going to go ahead with it soon." Dena's tone was firm.

Alex's heart leaped. He grabbed her hand, unable to stop himself. "Dena, thanks, thanks so much."

She didn't pull away, but squeezed back. "So it's you and me, partner."

She had a surprisingly soft touch for a gardener. He'd always figured her fingers would have calluses from work. He raised her hand so he could examine it.

The porch light shone softly through the stained glass pane decorating Dena's front door. The faceted glass, in the shape of a six-pointed star, formed myriad prisms that shed rainbows on their joined hands.

He kissed her palm. Her fingers, trembling, curled gently around his face, an unexpected caress that made his heart reel. He could hear her breath slip in and out through her moist, parted lips.

But kissing that sweet mouth wouldn't fill the hole in his soul.

He ached for all he'd lost. *Tamara.* He let Dena's hand drop but didn't release it.

"Good night, Alex," she whispered.

"Good night, Dena." His voice sounded rough, so he cleared his throat. "I'll call when I've set up the appointments."

"Okay. Umm…" Dena's tone had resumed its normal volume. "I don't think I should make a big deal about it with the twins. When I go to the doctor, I'll just tell them I'm going to see about a baby. They'll ask questions if they want to know anything, and I feel we should just answer them truthfully."

He nodded. "That's fine. They're your kids. You know what's best. But I appreciate your asking me what I think."

"I feel we should be on the same page about this." She smiled, which didn't entirely soften the blow when she tugged her hand out of his. She opened the door.

The night air, perfumed with the scents of Dena's garden, cooled and refreshed him, clearing his head. What had just happened? Had he nearly kissed Dena Randolph?

It must have been the wine.

He wasn't going to kiss his deceased wife's sister. Tamara hadn't been in her grave for even a year. This couldn't be right. Dena didn't even like him. They'd never gotten along.

True, he'd had a nice time tonight, but that wasn't enough to revise his opinion of her.

Was it?

Alex picked up his briefcase from the porch. He walked briskly to Tamara's Jag, then got in and drove away.

Dena closed the front door, then leaned against it, pressing a hand to her mouth. She didn't move until her heartbeat slowed to a normal pace.

What on earth had just happened? She'd been out of the single life for over a decade, since she met Steve Randolph. Steve's infidelities and abandonment had burned her to a crisp. Though divorced for close to five years, she hadn't dated.

She wasn't sure, but maybe, just maybe, Alex Chandler had wanted to kiss more than her hand. He'd been staring at her mouth as though it were a lollipop, ready to be licked.

A quiver danced through her body.

She bit her lip. She was nuts. Alex didn't like her. She didn't like Alex. Sure, they'd had a nice evening, but that was all it had been—nice. Not soul-shattering. No bells. No violins. The earth hadn't moved.

She and Tamara, the children of different fathers, had been complete opposites. If Alex preferred petite blondes, why would he want a tall redhead? *I'm imagining things…must have been the wine.*

Going to the living room, Dena picked up the half-full glasses. She dumped the wine into the kitchen sink, then went to the refrigerator and took out the open bottle of Chardonnay. If she was going to have an embryo implanted soon, she'd better clean out her house and her body of everything that could hurt the baby.

She poured the rest of the bottle down the drain, but decided to keep the four beers that remained from a six-pack in case Alex wanted one.

Opening the freezer, she removed a bag of espresso coffee. Her mom loved espresso, so Dena would take it to Irina's when she dropped off the twins the next morning.

Android Alex hadn't wanted to kiss her, and no way would she ever let him. They were totally unsuited for each other.

Dena's classy, dainty sister had fitted into the Chandler family like a Popsicle into a freezer. Dena believed that Alex's parents thought she was a cuckoo in Tamara's nest. Patricia and Leighton Chandler tolerated Irina because she was a celebrity, but Dena the gardener and her toddlers weren't a part of their restrained, immaculate world.

Dena opened a cupboard and took out a package of tea, setting it on the counter next to the espresso. She had to empathize with Alex's desire for the loving family that he'd missed. She'd been to the Chandlers' Pacific Heights mansion only once, to attend a reception in Alex and Tamara's honor. The Chandlers had disliked their elopement, but still wanted to present their son's beautiful, talented wife to the cream of San Francisco society.

Wincing, Dena recalled that Leighton and Patricia had proudly showed off their acquisitions, which they'd collected from all over the world. When Alex had greeted the family cook more warmly than he did his parents,

Dena realized that the Chandlers' travels had never included their only child.

Poor Alex. Dena pictured a lonely little boy, raised by
servants in that museum of a house.

Goldie pawed at the kitchen door, so Dena let the dog
in and stroked her pet's soft fur. Dena wanted her sister's
child reared with the love and sharing that she'd always
taken for granted. Now it seemed that Alex did also.
"Good for him," she said to the dog.

Chapter Five

"For heaven's sake, Alex, what's wrong?" Dena tentatively touched Alex's tense fingers, clenched into fists around the steering wheel of Tamara's silver Jag. His knuckles shone white. "Today's the big day. You oughtta be happy."

Alex stared forward, a fixed, taut expression on his face, as the brick-fronted clinic came into Dena's view. He turned into the underground parking lot and stopped the car. "I'm sorry. This place has a lot of bad memories for me."

"Ohhh. Is Tamara's oncologist in this building?" Unfastening the seat belt with a click, Dena opened her door and stepped out.

He halted in midstride at the hood of the car. "Yes. Plus, we tried to get pregnant here—oh, half a dozen times."

They walked toward the door of the clinic. Dread, a flannel-wrapped weight, settled around Dena's heart.

"Then she was diagnosed. Six months later, she died.

End of story.'' He opened the smoked-glass door for her. ''I hate this place.''

She touched his arm. ''There're other clinics. We can go somewhere else.''

Alex shook his head. ''Dr. Mujedin is a top infertility specialist. He wrote the book on in vitro fertilization.'' He turned to the left and began walking down a carpeted corridor.

Dena noticed a sign by the elevator reading Ob-Gyn, Second Floor. ''Hey, don't we have to go up?''

Stopping, he closed his eyes. A look of resignation crossed his face. ''Sorry. I was on automatic. She, uh, went for her chemo down this hall.''

Dena bit her lip. Absorbed with the problems of single motherhood—like paying her mortgage—she hadn't fully shared this aspect of Tamara's life. Unable to accept that her sister's disease could be fatal, Dena had believed they'd have more time together. Had she been selfish? And when would all these regrets end?

Maybe this new baby would help everyone make a fresh start.

The elevator arrived and they traveled up to the second floor, then walked down a quiet, carpeted hall. Alex opened a door decorated with colorful prints and cutout paper balloons, ushering Dena into the Ob-Gyn clinic. She sat while Alex approached the receptionist.

''Good morning, Mr. Chandler.'' Surprised, Dena realized that the grandmotherly looking woman remembered Alex although many months must have passed since his last visit.

''Hello, Mrs. Nakano.'' Apparently Alex recalled the receptionist. With a wince, Dena concluded that he and Tamara must have spent lots of time in this office.

Alex gestured. ''This is Ms. Randolph.''

"Very good. You're right on time. Mr. Chandler, take a seat. Ms. Randolph, come this way."

"Mr. Chandler?"

Alex recognized the tall woman with beaded cornrows and a friendly smile who joined him in the waiting room. She was Dr. Mujedin's colleague, an embryologist. "Yes, Dr. Fried?"

"You might want to join Ms. Randolph. Dr. Mujedin says she's a little anxious." She led him down the hall to a closed door before disappearing into her laboratory.

Despite the cool air, sweat beaded Alex's brow. He leaned against the wall outside the door and took out a folded linen square. He wiped his forehead. *Calm down,* he told himself. *She's fertile. She's healthy. This is going to be all right.* Tucking away the handkerchief, he tapped on the door and entered the room.

Dena lay prone on an examination table. She turned her head when he came in. "At last, Alex." Her voice was high with stress.

She appeared to be nearly naked under a sheet, with only a skimpy hospital gown giving extra coverage to the essential parts. Her hips were elevated higher than her head.

Alex's mouth went dry. "Uh, hi. How are you feeling?" His chest felt tight, and he couldn't speak easily.

"Like an idiot. I didn't expect this. Why does he have me with my tushie up in the air?"

"I don't know. I guess that makes the implantation easier. Didn't he explain the procedure?"

"Yes, he did, but he didn't get specific."

"Is there any way I can make you more comfortable?"

"Not really. Well, yeah. Can you find me a blanket?

I'm kinda cold, especially my feet.'' She wiggled her toes, which protruded from the end of the table.

He'd never before seen bossy Dena so helpless. He couldn't stop himself. He reached out and tickled one of her bare soles.

Dena squealed and kicked. ''Alex, you creep!''

Laughing, he scooted away. He found a blanket in a drawer and waved it in the air. ''No kicking, okay?''

''No tickling, okay?''

''Deal.'' He draped her with the fluffy white cover.

She sighed. ''This is taking forever.''

''Not really. The waiting just seems to last a long time.''

''Hey, isn't there even a radio?'' She craned her head.

''No, but there's music, sort of. Soothing stuff, obviously.'' He went to the white noise machine and flicked it on. The calming sound of waves washing over a beach filled the room.

Dena sighed again. ''You even know where they keep the zombie music.''

He sat on a chair near her head. ''Yes, I've been here a few times. Just relax. In a couple of minutes, the embryos will be ready. Then they'll implant them.''

''The things I've done for my sister,'' she said, with affectionate exasperation in her tone.

Alex twitched, anxious. ''If you resent the situation, maybe you shouldn't do this.''

''Oh, don't get me wrong. I feel fine about the baby. I love kids. Tamara couldn't have one, and you need one.'' Her voice softened. ''I know how important this is to you and Tami. This is…this is the last gift I can give my sister. I miss her, too, you know.''

''I know.'' He took her hand, feeling closer to her than ever before. He rubbed his finger along the top of her hand, appreciating her soft skin. Was she as soft and silky all over?

He froze. He dropped her hand. What had gotten into him lately? *Testosterone overload,* he thought. *A few games of pickup basketball should take care of this.*

The doctor bustled in, all white-coated efficiency. "Hello, Mr. Chandler. How are you feeling, Ms. Randolph?"

"Nervous." Dena shifted restlessly under the sheet. She did want to do this for her sister, but now she needed it over, fast. She thought she'd jump out of her skin, she was so scared. What was she getting into? Tension twisted her insides.

"Oh, there's nothing to be afraid of," Dr. Mujedin said. "This is an experimental procedure, but you'll be unhurt by it, whatever the outcome."

"What's new about it? I thought IVF was almost routine." She found herself chattering to relieve her anxiety.

"We are creating life, Ms. Randolph." Dr. Mujedin's face was serious. "This is never, ever routine, and it is always risk-laden for the embryos. The probability of implantation is only thirty percent for each one. That's why we'll insert three, and hope one survives."

"Oh, I'm very healthy." Dena wanted to persuade herself that she wouldn't need to go through this torment again. "Betcha I'll get pregnant first time out."

"I certainly hope you are right, Ms. Randolph." He picked up a speculum and a tube of lubricant from the counter.

Alex leaned forward to brush the hair off her forehead, startling her. "Dena, do you want me to leave?"

"Uh, yes. No. I don't know!" She needed someone, but could Android Alex help her through this?

"Whatever you want is okay," he murmured. "I was

here with Tamara, every time. Just close your eyes and try to relax."

She took a deep breath, then let it out slowly. "Okay. Stay. I guess."

"Please relax your legs, Ms. Randolph." The doctor moved the blanket up to her waist.

She tensed, but cooperated. Cool air washed her thighs. She pillowed her head on her crossed arms. *This is much worse than I thought.*

"Bear with me." She felt chill pressure against her as he began the procedure.

Alex touched her hair, caressing a strand. "It's okay," he whispered. "Tamara said that this was the worst part, but it's over soon."

"What did she say it felt like?" Fearfully, Dena watched as Dr. Mujedin took a long plastic tube before continuing. She closed her eyes. She couldn't watch.

"She said it felt like a little pinch and a pull, but not bad." Alex tucked a strand of hair behind her ear. "Just take deep breaths."

Dena felt a probing inside her and a cramping sensation. She involuntarily arched her back. Tears prickled behind her lids. Oh, God, no. She didn't want to cry. No.

"Easy," the doctor said. "You're doing great. The tough part's over now. Head back down, and please stay in that position." Rising, he pressed a button on the counter.

Alex stroked her cheek. His hand stopped when he touched the wetness on her face.

She smelled a faint whiff of his lime-sharp aftershave just before he kissed her tears away, his lips gentle. "It's okay," he whispered. "You're wonderful, sweetie. Just a few more minutes now."

As real and tender as the caress of his lips on her cheek, Alex's compassion overwhelmed her. She breathed deeply, eased by his calm voice and the unbelievable depth of his caring. Why had she never before seen his kindness?

She met his gaze, warm and blue as the summer sea. She wanted to sail with him into forever. In his eyes, she read the same concern and love she felt.

She knew he'd stay by her side. They'd travel together on this quest for Tamara's baby.

A tap sounded at the door just before a tall, heavyset woman in blue scrubs entered the room. Alex leaned back into his chair, still touching Dena's face.

"Dena, I'm Dr. Fried, your embryologist. We have three embryos for you today." The young doctor carried a tube attached to a syringe.

Dena's tension had reached a breaking point, and she tried not to giggle. Dr. Fried—what a name for an egg doctor—sounded matter-of-fact, as if she were announcing the menu choices at a restaurant. *We have three specials for your luncheon pleasure…*

Dr. Fried stepped behind Dena and announced, "I'm attaching this catheter to the plastic tube that Dr. Mujedin inserted into your uterus. A little push of the plunger and…there they go."

"Embryos transferred." Dr. Mujedin sounded a lot more serious than Dr. Fried.

"Bombs away." Dena giggled. She drew in another deep breath, warning herself that laughter might jiggle free the precious embryos.

To her surprise, Alex guffawed. "See ya later, boys."

"Or girls," Dena pointed out.

"True enough," Dr. Fried said. "We'll take either

sex. We're not picky here. Let's get Ms. Randolph to a flatter position.''

Dr. Mujedin pressed a button on the side of the table, which straightened. ''Roll over now and just relax.''

''You might as well take a nap.'' Dr. Fried walked to the door. ''You can't move for a couple of hours.''

Alex helped Dena slowly turn. ''Visualize our little guys—or girls—implanting.''

''Dream a little implant dream,'' Dr. Fried sang as she left.

Alone, Dena flattened her back against the table and tried to rest. Though it was padded, she couldn't get comfortable.

Far from drowsy, she still trembled from the enormity of the event she'd just undergone. If they'd been lucky, they'd made a life.

More amazing had been Alex's response to it.

Alex. She remembered the intensity in his blue eyes as he caressed her, easing her distress. He acted as though she was the center of his world, that nothing else mattered but her.

She shivered. *No wonder Tamara was so in love with him,* she thought. Dena had never before understood the attraction between her half sister and Alex. Now Dena saw his compassion.

Far from being a chilly Chandler, Alex had radiated concern and kindness. When he'd kissed away her tears, her surprise had completely distracted her from the procedure. Remembering his unexpected tenderness made her want to…want to…

She wanted to kiss him back, really kiss him. Not a

chaste, sister-to-brother-in-law kiss. A real kiss, with lips and teeth and tongues and a full-body hug. The works.

She tore her mind away from the thought. No matter what she might feel, Alex didn't care about her. He wanted this baby. She was just the vessel. *And that's okay,* she reminded herself. *This is Alex and Tamara's child,* not mine.

Closing her eyes, Dena visualized a tiny baby getting stuck to the side of her uterus. The baby had Alex's chiseled good looks and a little lock of blond hair. She smiled at the idea of a mini-Alex growing inside her.

But she found it hard to imagine a baby who didn't exist, when the real Alex Chandler, moments ago, had comforted her so sweetly. There'd been true affection in his gentle touch.

She wanted more.

Her nipples tightened, the hard little buds scraping against the starched sheet under which she lay. A sexual heat flooded her body.

What would Alex be like in bed? Would some of that intensity she'd glimpsed explode when he made love?

Would she ever find out?

Dena's eyes popped open when she realized the turn her half-awake, half-asleep dreams had taken.

I am having a sexual fantasy about Alex Chandler.

I want Alex Chandler to make love with me.

Dena rubbed her face with both hands. She was certifiable. Not only did she want her deceased sister's husband—which couldn't be right—but she'd just undergone a procedure to make her pregnant. If everything happened as planned, in a few months she'd look like a beach ball. There was no question, none, about starting a romance with anyone.

She was crazy, no doubt about it. Did they put expectant mothers in straitjackets? She hoped not.

Any relationship she started right now was doomed. So she wouldn't start one. Period.

The twins and this new baby deserved her total attention. Besides, after the drubbing Steve had given her ego and her heart, Dena didn't know if she was ready for romance. She'd accepted she might *never* be ready.

Also, Alex might never be ready. *He's still mourning Tamara,* she told herself. *Forget about him.*

Emotionally exhausted, Alex retreated to one of the armchairs in the waiting room. Slumping in it, he closed his eyes.

He couldn't forget the look on Dena's face during the procedure. She'd reminded him of Tamara, showing the same mixture of awe and fear, bolstered by sheer gutsiness. Her courage startled him, but lately, Dena had shown him depths of character he hadn't known existed. She'd even managed to crack a joke and giggle at that offbeat Dr. Fried.

Perhaps he'd misjudged Dena in the past. He'd never understood the bond between his wife and her sister, thinking them polar opposites. Now he saw their similarities. They shared determination, spirit and intelligence.

His child would be lucky. Both mothers, biological and surrogate, were special women.

How close should the baby be to Dena? In making this decision, Alex knew he held all the cards. The contract Dena had signed assured him of control. But his outlook had changed. He'd observed that Dena was a good mother. And the implant procedure hadn't been easy for her, but when the going got tough, she'd stood fast through her fear.

Though not without a tear or two. Kissing her tears away—from where had that impulse come? He didn't know, but caring for her seemed so natural, so right. Better, she hadn't flinched from his touch.

Could Dena's feelings toward him have changed, also?

Alex shifted restlessly in his chair. He wasn't entirely comfortable with the intimacy they'd shared during the implant. They were family—sort of—and he didn't like his attraction to her. *It's just hormones, Alex. Get used to it. And stop looking at her body!*

He'd have to make sure that Tamara's baby developed a healthy relationship with Dena without getting too close to her. Tall order, but he'd find a way.

A door opened and Dena, looking refreshed from her nap, entered the waiting room. Dressed in her customary jeans and T-shirt, she didn't meet his gaze as she stalked to the door. "Ready to go?" she asked.

He pointed to a paper bag she carried. "What's that?"

She winced. "Progesterone suppositories."

"Oh, lovely."

They both laughed.

"What are they for?" he asked, opening the door for her.

"Dr. Fried said that they'll strengthen the uterine lining to keep the implants in place. I need to get more at the pharmacy." She marched down the hall, her stride loose-limbed and swift.

"I'll take care of that for you." He hurried after Dena. What was with her? During the procedure, they'd been so close, even intimate. Now she acted as though she'd become one of the chilly Chandlers. He wanted to pull back, too, but what was her problem?

She paused, pushing the button to call the elevator. "That's okay. I can deal with it myself."

"You don't have to. I'm here to take care of you."

"I'm becoming pregnant, Alex, not disabled. I don't need you or anyone to take care of me." The elevator had arrived, so she stepped in.

She might as well have slapped him in the face. "You don't understand. If you don't stay quiet, the embryos won't implant." Entering the elevator, he pushed the down button.

She sagged against the wall. "You're right."

He wondered what he could say to make this horrible tension dissolve. "Look, I know you're not used to depending on a man, but I'm not Steve. I'm not going anywhere."

She tensed, as though she wanted to flee from the elevator, which had now stopped at the ground floor. "You're right. You're right about everything." She sucked in a breath. "I'm sorry."

"You don't need to be sorry, either." He grabbed her hand and held it as they walked to the car. "This isn't about being right or being sorry. This is about having a very special baby."

She squeezed his hand, then let it go. "This is hard for me to get used to."

"What?"

"You. Being here. So much a part of my life. You always seemed so remote."

He shrugged, then pawed in his pocket for the car keys. "I was pretty wrapped up with Tamara."

''Now I'm the focus of all that attention.'' She shivered as she reached for the door handle.

He beat her to it, opening the door for her. ''Get used to me. You're carrying three of my kids, and I'm not going anywhere.''

Chapter Six

"Guess what, Alex." Dena carried two glasses of lemonade to the farmhouse table in her kitchen, then put one in front of Alex. Her smile teased his nerve endings.

"What?" He could hear the shouts of the twins at play outside in the balmy May sunshine.

"I think I'm pregnant. Actually, I'm pretty sure."

"Yeah? Wow!" He wasn't prepared for the joy bursting through his system. He jumped up from his chair, tipping it over, and hugged Dena.

She squeezed back, her eyes a little wet. He impulsively kissed her tears away, just as he'd done at the doctor's office a few weeks earlier. She hadn't minded then, and she didn't object now.

He stopped and stared at her, abruptly shattered by a thought. She didn't look any different. "Are you sure?"

She pulled away. "Hey, I've been pregnant before. Sure, I'm sure. The pregnancy test will confirm what I already know."

"Well, here's your payoff—or part of it." He opened his wallet and took out a check.

"I'm not doing it for the money, Alex." She took a bag of tortilla chips from the cupboard and emptied them into a blue ceramic bowl.

"I know you're not, but you haven't been able to work since the implantation. This should help. Ummm, have you thought of replacing your pickup?"

Dena glanced at the check. "Oh, this isn't enough to buy a truck. This'll go to pay bills." She opened a jar of salsa and dug into it with a chip.

"That reminds me." Alex went to the cupboards, peeking into each. He didn't like what he saw—or, rather, what he didn't see. "Dena, where are your pre-natal vitamins?"

"Hey, you can ask. You don't need to go spying." She sounded annoyed. "Sit back down, okay?"

"What have you been eating lately?" Back at the table, he glowered at her snack. "Chips and salsa aren't a balanced diet."

"True enough. But I ate a can of tuna about an hour ago."

"A whole can?"

"Yeah. Got a craving for protein."

"Is that normal?" He sipped his lemonade, which had just the right combo of sweet and tart flavors.

Dena shrugged. "You know the stories about pregnant women. Some want pickles and ice cream. I like tuna, chips and salsa. Salty and spicy food." She grinned at him impishly. "And then I throw up."

Alex choked on his drink. "Thank you for the warning. Should I move out of range?"

She leaned back in her chair and roared with laughter.

Not a sweet, dainty, ladylike giggle, like something Tamara might have emitted, but a full-throated Dena laugh.

He liked it, and liked her even though she was as different from her sister—her *half* sister—as chopped liver from fine pate.

"What are we going to tell my parents?" he asked her.

"You haven't told them?" Her eyes widened. "I'm expecting their grandchild and they don't know?"

"I didn't want to get their hopes up." He gestured with his lemonade glass. "You know what I mean. The doctor still isn't sure you're pregnant."

"Oh, I'm preggers all right. Can't you tell by my diet?" Dena snickered. "I bet you don't want to try to explain to your parents that your sister-in-law the gardener is having your baby by Tamara."

Alex wasn't proud of his parents' high-society, snobby attitudes. Sacramento's excellent business climate aside, he'd moved away from San Francisco to escape Leighton and Patricia. "You have to admit that my mother isn't going to take it well. She won't like becoming a grandmother."

With five face-lifts and a hair-dye addiction, Alex's mother fought aging tooth and nail.

"And what will her friends say? Surrogate motherhood as social solecism. I can just see Patricia now." Dena pitched her voice high, giving it his mother's artificial accent. "But Alexander, darling, I'm sure that nothing like this has happened in The Family before."

"We have to tell them something, sometime." He sat next to her. "They're going to Blanche and Greg's wedding. Will you show by late July?"

"Bet on it. I'm already wearing my baggy jeans. In

July I'll be big as a blimp.'' She crunched a chip loaded with salsa.

''That soon?''

''Yeah. Last time, it took a few months for me to show. I guess because it's my second pregnancy, my stomach muscles gave up right away.''

Alex frowned. He didn't see many pregnant women at public or business events. He wasn't a prig, but he believed women should take extra care of themselves at such a sensitive time in their lives. ''Are you sure it's all right for you to go to the wedding?''

Dena stared at him, wide-eyed. ''Of course.''

He stood to go to the phone. ''I'm going to check with Dr. Mujedin.''

''Alex, don't be ridiculous.''

Ignoring her, he poked the familiar numbers on the phone's buttons.

''Give me that phone.'' Dena grabbed it from his hand. ''I know how to be pregnant. You don't have to check with the doctor about every little thing.''

''This isn't a usual pregnancy.''

''Don't be such an alarmist.''

''We don't even know for sure if there's an implant.''

''I'm telling you, I'm pregnant. Can't you trust me?''

He leaned against the counter. ''This is going to be a long nine months if you constantly argue.''

''This is going to be a long nine months if you don't calm down.'' She stood less than a foot from him, arms akimbo, hands on her hips. The position made her breasts strain against her T-shirt. Had they become bigger since implantation? He hoped so. Weren't larger breasts a symptom of pregnancy?

He jerked his gaze to her eyes, which now flashed

with anger. "You have my embryos in your body, Dena. I expect you to respect my opinion."

"I'm a mother, Alex. I expect you to respect my experience." Dena pointed to the door. "Out."

"What?"

"Door's that way."

"You're throwing me out?" He'd better check the contract. Could she do this?

"I don't want to argue with you. Stress is bad for the baby. We can talk about this some other time."

Alex flinched at the thought of harm to his child. "I'm sorry. You're absolutely right." He dashed to the door. "I'll call when I've talked to the doctor."

She pressed her full lips together into a tight, flat line.

"You stay calm and happy now, all right?" Alex quietly closed the door behind him, then waved goodbye to the twins.

As he fumbled in his pocket for the car keys, he berated himself for upsetting Dena. Pregnant women behaved strangely from hormones, and she was ingesting extra hormones to assure implantation. He ought to be more patient and understanding with the mother of his baby during this difficult time.

She needed serenity, space and calmness in her life. She didn't need him gawking at her chest and fighting about the pregnancy. He'd get Dr. Mujedin to talk with Dena about proper conduct for the next nine months.

Inside the house, Dena rubbed her sweating face with a dish towel and mentally cussed herself out for exploding at Alex. *Darn hormones.* Off balance since the implantation procedure, she blamed herself for the quarrel. She'd been pregnant before and knew what to expect. She should have anticipated her moods.

But everything was different, not just her body. Her

feelings about Alex had transformed, and Dena didn't like it at all. Her world had tilted on its axis. She loathed the sense of disorientation.

But Dena hated unfairness. And because she didn't lack courage, she trotted to the door to wave her hand at the Jag before Alex drove away.

Too late. Dena slowly turned away from the door, wondering how on earth she could make amends.

A few days later, on a sunny Sunday morning, Alex, stripped to the waist, jogged along the American River Parkway. The paved trail—a bike path with jogging lanes on either side—ran some thirty miles from Discovery Park in north Sacramento, to Folsom in the southeast. When Tami was alive and healthy, they'd sometimes ride their bikes all the way, using Dena's home, about midway through the route, as a pit stop.

Today, Alex hadn't intended to halt at all, but the morning turned warm and he quickly drained his water bottle. Leaving the path at Goethe Park, which everyone in Sacramento called ''Getty,'' he increased his speed to a sprint as he approached Dena's home. Drenched with sweat, he staggered to the front door at about nine o'clock, grabbing a post for support while he caught his breath.

He didn't know what kind of reception he'd receive. He hadn't seen Dena since she'd seen fit to throw him out of her house. But he didn't have any other reasonable choices, and he hoped that no matter how mad Dena had been, she'd cooled down and seen the error of her ways. She wouldn't refuse him a drink of water and a visit to the bathroom.

A tap on the front door brought no response, except from Goldie. The retriever sniffed Alex's legs with interest. When Alex patted her on the head, she licked a trail of sweat running down his forearm. Alex grimaced.

With Goldie following, he walked to the back door, the one that opened onto the kitchen. He could hear the twins' clear, high voices, so he knocked on the door and rattled the knob.

The twins immediately fell silent.

He knocked again.

"We're not supposed to open the door without Mommy." Alex recognized Miriam's voice, edged with suspicion.

"It's Uncle Alex, Miri."

"Unka Alex, Unka Alex!" The door flew open amid excited shrieks and chatter.

Alex smelled the lingering aroma of cooked food. Last night's dinner? He looked around, seeing smoke rising from the toaster.

"Pipe down, Miri!" Jack whispered. "You'll wake Mommy."

"She's probably awake already," Miri said, but in a quieter tone. Her tiny hands dragged Alex inside.

"What's going on here?" he asked. Striding to the toaster, he poked a button. Toast the color of charcoal popped up.

"Don't!" Miriam grabbed his hand. "That's Mommy's breakfast!"

"Where's your mother?"

"Sleeping," Jack said. "It's Mother's Day, so we turned off her alarm clock."

"We're making Mommy a special breakfast." Miriam went to a low cupboard and removed a tray, then arranged a blue-and-white gingham napkin on one side.

Though touched by the twins' thoughtfulness, Alex

decided he'd better supervise or the kids would torch the house. "Umm, has anyone fed the dog?"

Jack looked shamefaced. So did Miri. "We forgot," she whispered. "I'm sorry, Goldie." She hugged the retriever around the neck, burying her face in Goldie's fur.

"We were thinking about Mom. I'll do it. C'mon, Goldie." Jack scampered to the door and flung it open. With a clatter and scratch of paws, the dog followed, tail waving. Jack swung the door back.

Alex caught the door before it could slam shut and rattle the entire house. "Bring back a flower for Mommy's tray." *Might as well do it up right.*

Jack stopped, cocking his head as though considering the novel request. "Okay."

Alex turned. "Get a fork and spoon for Mommy, Miriam."

Fifteen minutes later, they'd prepared a tray for Dena with orange juice, fresh toast and scrambled eggs. Jack had picked a pink rose, and Miriam had arranged it on the gingham napkin. Though the twins remained excited, Alex had persuaded them to nibble on toast and eat a few bites of egg.

Alex headed toward the bathroom. Out of respect for Dena, he wanted to towel off before taking her tray to her.

Miriam stopped him. "That one's broke, Unka Alex."

"Broken, Miri?"

"Yeah. You gotta use the one up there." Miri pointed up the stairs.

"Okay." Alex leaped up the steps in several bounds. Jogging had given him lots of energy.

The door of the second floor bathroom was shut. From

behind it came the sound of running water and Jack's voice singing tuneless notes vaguely resembling a song.

Alex stopped, undecided, and glanced at Dena's closed bedroom door. He didn't want to disturb her but figured he could slip in, use her bathroom, and sneak out again.

He tapped on her door, eased it ajar, then peeked inside.

Dena slept, her face turned away from him. Lit by the sun filtering through the lace curtains, her red hair spread on her pillow like a sunset cloud, satiny-soft, lush and touchable.

The muscles in Alex's lower belly tightened. He imagined digging his hands into the enticing, silken mass.

He opened the door so he could edge through. Its hinges creaked and squealed.

Dena sat up in bed, eyes popping open. The sheet covering her slid down to her waist, exposing the most beautiful breasts Alex had seen in a *very* long time.

Their gazes met. Dena screamed and grabbed for the sheet.

Yelping, Alex jerked around. The sight of Dena's full, creamy pair, tipped by pointed, dusky rose nipples, completely undid him. He scrambled for escape and whacked into the doorpost. He fell into the hall on his butt, clutching his forehead.

Jack, who'd emerged from the bathroom, howled with laughter.

"Pipe down. Alex? Are you all right?" In the midst of the tumult, Dena's voice sounded surprisingly calm.

Totally humiliated, he dizzily regarded the baseboards. Could he crawl underneath them?

"Alex, it's okay. Jackie, help Uncle Alex."

Reassured by her serene tone, Alex collected himself and found Jack by his side, staring at him with round, anxious eyes. "Are you okay, Uncle Alex? I'm sorry I laughed."

Alex tentatively fingered his head. "It's all right. I would have laughed, too."

"You sure woulda." Jack grinned. "You looked just like a cartoon."

Alex envisioned stars spinning around his head. "Gee, thanks, buddy."

After his skull quit clanging, Alex fetched the breakfast tray and returned to Dena's bedroom. Now robed in her pink chenille, she sat in an armchair by the window. Averting his eyes from her neckline, Alex placed the tray onto a small, round table in front of her. Miriam crowded close to her mother, and Dena lovingly ruffled her daughter's dark hair.

"Darling, this is so sweet of you. And you, too, Alex."

Alex relaxed. She hadn't held a grudge about their last, unfortunate, meeting. Even better, she didn't seem to be startled or embarrassed by his inadvertent view of her breasts.

Focused on her children, Dena was hugging the kids, her eyes a little teary. Thinking he might be intruding, he said, "Uh, I'll just go—"

"Oh, no!" Dena stretched out an arm toward him. The opening of her robe shifted at the chest, giving him a tiny glimpse of the sweet curves beneath. "You don't have to leave."

He took her extended hand before he thought about it. She clasped him warmly.

A tremor zipped up his arm to his heart. Then heat arrowed southward. This is a mistake, he thought. But he couldn't just drop her hand, not when they were getting along so well. He didn't want to upset her, he told himself. It had nothing to do with how good her fingers felt, nestled within his grasp. Certainly the memory of her lovely breasts didn't enter into his thinking at all.

Looking around, he wasn't sure he wanted to be there. The place assailed his emotions on so many levels.

The queen-size bed that occupied the middle of the room was covered by a hand-pieced quilt and rumpled white sheets. Had Steve and Dena conceived the twins on that bed?

An image of Dena, hot and panting, writhing on the mattress, filled his brain, but Steve wasn't the male in the scenario. Instead, Alex—

Stop it, Alex!

Squeezing Dena's hand, he gently disengaged his own.

"Everyone sit on the bed while I eat. You too, Alex." Dena picked up her fork and began on her eggs. "This is so great. Thank you, everybody. Kids, did you have any breakfast? Alex?"

"I fed the twins. But I don't usually eat while I'm running." Alex perched gingerly on the edge of Dena's bed. Jack and Miriam bounced onto the mattress near him, totally at ease.

"I figured that's what you were doing." Dena scanned his bare torso, then returned to her meal.

Her lids had dropped over her expressive green eyes, so he couldn't tell if she was checking him out, or just…looking.

"Why aren't you in San Francisco, Alex? Where are your parents?"

"They're away." Alex wanted to change the subject. His mother hadn't enjoyed parenthood or anything associated with it, including Mother's Day. And when he and Tamara had been together, trying to make a baby, Mother's Day had become another occasion for scheduled lovemaking. The day had always been followed by the disappointing news that Tami hadn't conceived. Alex asked, "Why aren't you with Irina?"

Dena continued eating, unruffled by his attempt to turn the tables. "We usually take an early supper over to her house on Mother's Day. That way the twins can swim in her pool, but Mom doesn't have to do any work."

Miriam's warm weight cuddled against Alex's side, but before she could settle down, Jack bonked his sister on the head with a pillow. Miri, no pushover, immediately retaliated, and the bed became a battleground.

Nibbling on the last piece of toast, Dena curled up in her chair and watched Alex roughhouse with the twins.

She enjoyed the comfort of her family close by. With a jolt, she realized that Alex had become part of the equation. He was family.

That cozy warmth combined with a sexy sizzle, the product of watching Alex's naked torso at close range. And he'd seen more of her than ever before. She'd never forget his expression when he'd glimpsed her breasts. His eyes had practically fallen out of his face while his jaw had dropped to the floor. His look of startled amazement had been more flattering than ten dozen red roses.

Now her chaotic emotions clashed inside her, producing a weird, unsettled feeling unlike anything Dena had previously experienced.

He might be family, yes, but no other family member had a body like Alex's. She'd assumed that a fit body dwelt beneath his staid, three-piece suits, but the reality blew away her most explicit fantasies. Alex was gorgeous, with buffed pecs dusted with a fine golden down, a six-pack worthy of an Olympic athlete, and sinewy, muscular legs.

Alex was a hunk.

Dena curved her hand around her stomach, protective of the new life growing within. When she'd become pregnant with the twins, she'd dreamed of family scenes like this one. But those illusions had been inhabited by dark-haired, smiling Steve, her steady boyfriend, first lover and, eventually, the opponent in their divorce.

Steve had left. Would Alex?

Who could say? Tamara had found Alex good husband material. Her half sister and her husband had been deliriously happy until Tami couldn't conceive a child, and then had fallen so sick. Everything had crashed down around them. Sort of like the way her life had imploded, Dena reflected.

Dena felt a rueful smile on her lips. Battered survivors of unbelievable emotional turmoil, she and Alex had a lot in common.

But could it be enough?

Dena stomped down her dreams, reminding herself that to Alex, she was nothing more than the repository for his and Tamara's fetus. Doubtless after she gave birth, Alex would grab his baby and run far, far away.

Chapter Seven

Dena's heart gave an excited little jump when the silver Jag entered her driveway. When the doorbell rang, she dashed for her purse. She padded with quick, nervous steps to let Alex in. On this Tuesday afternoon, Alex was dressed in one of his sober, navy three-piece suits, with no concession to the sultry June weather.

Too bad, Dena thought. She wouldn't mind seeing a little more of Alex than his suit allowed. The running shorts he'd worn on Mother's Day exposed about the right amount of flesh, she decided.

"You look nice," he said, without enthusiasm in his voice. "I don't see you in a skirt very often."

What was wrong with him? Maybe he was nervous about the ultrasound.

Dena smoothed her long denim garment. "Uh, a skirt is better for an ultrasound than jeans. I'm kinda uncomfortable, if you know what I mean." The doctor had reminded her that, for good test results, she needed a full bladder.

He raised a brow. "Yes, I know."

"Been there, done that, huh?" She followed him to the car.

He opened the door for her. "In a manner of speaking." Walking to the driver's side, he slipped behind the wheel.

A memory of Tamara, distraught and weeping after a negative ultrasound, shot through Dena's mind. She winced. "I'm sorry. I didn't mean to bring up unpleasant memories." She tried to settle into the leather seat.

"Hopefully we'll have a happy ending. Do you still think you're pregnant?" Alex turned out of her driveway onto Shadownook.

"Well, the blood work came back positive, but they can make mistakes with those tests. I feel pregnant, but seeing the baby on the ultrasound will be a comfort."

"Yeah." Dena heard volumes of stress in that sighed word. He scrutinized the passing cars on Fair Oaks Boulevard before he turned left into the traffic.

Yes, Alex was definitely anxious about today's visit to Dr. Mujedin. Dena didn't know what to say to break the awful tension, so she stayed quiet. Neither uttered more than a phrase or two until she left Alex in the waiting room of Dr. Mujedin's office.

After changing into a hospital gown, she lay on the cushioned table in one of the examination rooms. Dr. Fried hovered while Dr. Mujedin smoothed a special gel over Dena's bare stomach to facilitate the ultrasound test.

"Shouldn't Alex be here?" Dena asked. "I thought he wanted to come in after I'd changed." *Not that he hasn't seen most of me already.*

"You're right. I'll get him." Dr. Fried went to the door.

Dena squirmed at the touch of the chill, flat instrument that Dr. Mujedin slid over her lower belly.

"Bear with me," he said. "Just another moment or two while I find your uterus."

"I'm sure it's there," Dena babbled. "I used it just four years ago to have twins."

She heard a tap on the door before it opened to admit Alex, followed by Dr. Fried.

Alex immediately rushed to Dena to stroke her hair. "How is she?" he asked Dr. Mujedin.

"Fine, fine. See? Here we are." Dr. Mujedin sounded pleased. "Looks like you have two implants. Congratulations, Mr. Chandler, you're going to be a father."

Alex slumped against the wall, audibly trying to inhale. Tugging a handkerchief out of his pocket, he rubbed his eyes. "Two?"

"Two? I'm going to have twins *again?*" Dena craned her head to see the flat, black-and-white screen. "Are you sure?"

"Maybe not." Dr. Fried leaned over to adjust the ultrasound screen. "You had the settings off-kilter, Albert," she said to Dr. Mujedin.

When Dena saw a tiny, blurred double image blend into one, she breathed a sigh of relief.

"Let me see him!" Alex crowded close to the screen. "So where is it?"

Dr. Fried pointed at a blob. "There's your bouncing baby…whatever. We can't tell the gender yet."

"We don't want to know," Alex and Dena chorused, before Dena looked at Alex and laughed, giddy with pleasure.

Dr. Fried pressed a button. A sheet of paper issued from the machine. "Had you going there, didn't he?" She winked at Dena.

"You're not kidding. I love my kids, but their birth was the pits. I was huge, and everything, from nursing to diapering through toilet training, seemed twice as difficult, compared to what other mothers have told me."

"I'm sure Mr. Chandler will help out." Dr. Fried nodded at Alex.

"Oh, yeah. Every second." Alex jiggled up and down, vibrating with tension. Dena stared at him, mystified.

Dr. Fried handed Alex the printout. He took it from her with shaky fingers.

"I'll make another for you, Ms. Randolph, while you change into your clothes," Dr. Fried said as Alex left.

"What's with him?" Dena asked.

"Oh, I see this often." Dr. Fried smiled. "He's been through the wringer with the infertility treatments. He doesn't believe it's really happening, and now that it is, he's terrified it will all go away."

Back in the waiting room, Alex sat and waited for Dena to emerge. Stunned, he couldn't quite believe what he'd just seen. The ultrasound result in his right hand fluttered to the floor as he again groped for his handkerchief.

Dena was pregnant. On the first try, he and Dena had implanted Tamara's baby. He reached down for the paper and stared at the triangular, black-and-white blur on it. His heart swelled until it threatened to burst from his chest.

His baby. This was his baby. He dabbed his moist eyes with the linen square. He was going to be a father.

He cautioned himself that many things could happen between this moment and January, when the baby was due. Sometimes babies conceived through IVF were premature. He dropped his head into his hands and prayed for the safety of his child. Alex added Dena into his thoughts when he realized that the surest road to the health of his baby would be through her.

Where was she? He wanted to share this moment with her. He wanted desperately to hold and touch the mother of his child. But what would be the repercussions of a closer relationship with Dena?

Drawing in a breath, Alex consciously willed his racing heartbeat to calm. Then he took a small pad of paper and a pen from the inside pocket of his suit. He had a good memory, but sometimes writing helped him sort out his thoughts.

Flipping open the pad to a fresh page, he wrote: *Dena—Pros and Cons.*

He began two lists. On the "con" side, he wrote "surrogate mother." Ouch. Any kind of intimacy with the surrogate mother of his child was asking for trouble. What if the relationship ended in disaster? Dena wouldn't deliberately harm the baby, but emotional distress could harm the developing fetus.

And what if Dena wanted to be closer to the child because of their friendship? An icy vise clenched around Alex's heart. He wouldn't risk a custody battle. This was *his* baby.

On the "pro" side, he wrote "honest." Trustworthy Dena wouldn't break her word. She understood the importance of this child to him.

Alex knew he'd taken a big risk in trying to have a baby by a surrogate. Gary had warned him of the hazards many times. Some surrogate mothers tried to keep the baby they'd borne.

The way Dena often caressed her belly suggested possessiveness, and her joy at the news they'd just received seemed a bit too maternal. He didn't like it.

But Dena hadn't only made a commitment to him. She honored her sister's memory by carrying her child.

Alex drew a star next to "honesty." Dena would never let him down.

On the "con" side, he scribbled, "life always seems to be a mess." But maybe that wasn't her fault. Raising twins alone, without their father, couldn't be easy. Alex decided that he should sympathize rather than criticize Dena for the way she faced her challenges. He'd judged her too harshly in the past.

Back to the "pro" side. "Reasonably attractive."

Who was he trying to fool? Labeling Dena "reasonably attractive" was like calling Tiger Woods a pretty good golfer. Dena was a knockout. Lush red hair he wanted to sink his fingers into. A curvy, sensuous body he ached to caress.

Since he'd seen a glimpse of her breasts on Mother's Day, he couldn't get her body out of his thoughts and dreams. How would those lovely globes feel cupped in his palms? Alex groaned and adjusted his pants.

With kissable lips and striking green eyes set in a face gilded by the sun, she didn't resemble Tamara much. She had her own special beauty. The half sisters had their mother's high cheekbones, and Irina, in her fifties, still turned men's heads.

On the other hand, wasn't "appearance" a part of beauty? Alex frowned. Tamara had been a perfect wife in so many ways. Alex's accounting partnership demanded that Tamara grace his arm at numerous business and social events. He couldn't picture earth mother Dena in a cocktail suit and heels at a chamber of commerce mixer or a political fund-raiser.

Perhaps he was wrong. Maybe he should give her a chance. He snapped his fingers, remembering that he and Dena would both participate in Greg and Blanche's wedding. Then he'd see if Dena could—

What was he thinking? That Dena could be his wife? The pad and pen dropped from his nerveless fingers.

This was indecent. Tamara hadn't been dead a year and he was thinking about replacing her—with her own sister, no less.

But he couldn't stop caring about the woman who carried his child. That was all right, wasn't it?

Late in July, Alex waited at the entrance of the Radisson Hotel, the site of Greg's wedding, watching his parents' gold Mercedes slow to a stop nearby. His tall, silver-haired father, clad in a tuxedo, got out and tossed the keys to a valet with a grin.

After shaking his father's hand, Alex opened the car door for his mother. Patricia's beige hair and manicured fingernails matched the trim on her taupe silk dinner suit.

"Mother."

"Alexander, darling." Lightly leaning upon his elbow, she stepped out of the car.

He stooped to kiss his mother's scented, suede-soft cheek. With her elbow linked through his, he accompanied his parents to the crowded ballroom where Greg and Blanche's wedding ceremony would take place. Decorated with pink roses in lavish floral swags and displays, the room rapidly filled with guests.

Alex eyed his mother. *How am I going to tell them?* he wondered. Ever since Dena had raised the thorny issue, he'd pondered the question like an auditor with a convoluted tax return. Despite her mockery, he knew she'd pegged his parents with absolute accuracy.

No doubt his parents would see his baby, borne by a surrogate mother, as an undesirable scientific experiment rather than a grandchild. His mother's first thought would be *How am I going to tell my friends?* His father would retreat to a tumbler of Scotch rather than face his mother's complaints about Alex's conduct.

"What is it, Alexander?" his mother asked.

He guided her to a chair. "Nothing, Mother."

His father looked at Alex. "Still miss Tami, son?" Understanding glimmered in Leighton's eyes.

"Yes, I do." Alex gazed at the glittering throng, dressed in tuxedos and gowns for the evening event. "But if we'd had a formal wedding it would be worse. I've never been happier that we eloped."

His mother clenched her jaw. She hadn't approved of their casual nuptials. *So what?* He gave her a big grin, just to get her goat. Mom needed to be shaken up a little.

"Excuse me. I'm supposed to seat other guests. I'll see you later, at the reception." Alex returned to the ballroom entrance. Soon, no empty chairs remained.

Slipping into his assigned place, Alex looked for Dena in the crowd of women. Dressed in floral-printed, low-cut gowns with long skirts, the bridesmaids looked like a pink flower bed. He couldn't see his quarry among them.

Worry tensed his spine. Where was she?

Back in the ballroom, a harpist started some wedding music that sounded vaguely familiar. Ushers matched themselves with bridesmaids, and the pairs began to walk up the aisle in time to the tune.

Alex went to his partner's side. "Greg, where are they?"

A frown etched a line between the groom's dark brows. "I don't know. The bride, the maid of honor and the matron of honor are…are…somewhere. I don't know where.'' He turned to look at a door. ''They're probably in the women's room. Isn't that where they hide out?''

Dena emerged from the women's lounge. Clad in the same gown as the rest of the females in the wedding party, she approached in a swish of flowered silk. A demure bolero jacket didn't quite cover her ample cleavage. Alex couldn't help admiring the view.

Swept into a French twist, her Titian hair gleamed. Curls had escaped the updo to charmingly frame her face. The pink flowered dress flattered her golden tan. She held a bouquet of roses in gloved hands. The gown didn't quite hide her belly, where *his* baby was growing to term.

Heart thudding, he resisted the impulse to cup her stomach. He knew he couldn't feel his baby kick yet— it was too early—but he eagerly awaited the day. He desperately wanted to feel the new life flourishing inside Dena.

''Greg, you have to get into that ballroom,'' Dena said. ''Blanche won't come out until you leave. She truly believes it's bad luck if the groom sees the bride before the ceremony.''

''Guess it's time.'' Greg tapped the arm of his brother, the best man. ''We'll go in, then Alex and Dena, then maybe the butterfly will emerge from the chrysalis.''

Alex hesitated. He didn't want to touch Dena in his current mood. He hadn't been entirely truthful to his parents. This wedding was making him feel dangerously emotional, especially around Dena, the woman who carried his baby. If he even took her elbow, he'd want to hold her tight. If he embraced her—well, there was no predicting what he'd do.

''Hey, am I supposed to be on the right or the left?''
Dena slipped her arm through his. He clasped her to his
side possessively.

''You're fine.'' The wedding consultant whispered to
the groom, ''Mr. Holloway, wait for the matron of honor
and her escort to enter first. I'll make sure the bride gets
in, all right?''

Alex nodded to Dena and they entered the ballroom.
He tried to look away, but her beauty kept his gaze
pinned to her profile. The pink lipstick on her full mouth
matched the flowers on her dress and the roses decorating the room. The blossoms' fragrance filled the air as
he paced the length of the aisle, holding Dena's elbow.

The white satin glove covering her forearm felt
smooth, sensuous under his fingers. He caressed the slick
material and felt a responsive tension in her muscles. He
gave her one last squeeze just before she pulled away.
With a flush rising in her cheeks, she took her place in
the line of female wedding attendants.

Greg and his brother entered just before the harpist
plucked ''Here Comes the Bride.''

Blanche, dressed in a similar gown of pure white,
swept up the aisle behind her maid of honor. Though his
partner's bride looked lovely, Alex preferred to watch
Dena's expressive face as the ceremony began. What
could she be thinking?

Dena eased her feet out of the uncomfortable, high-
heeled sandals Blanche had decreed the brides' attendants wear. A hundred bucks shot on stiletto-heeled tor-
ture chambers that Dena would never willingly put on
her feet again.

Because of her failed marriage with Steve, Dena hated
weddings. But tonight, the minister seemed to be moving

briskly, so this one would be over soon. Even so, she couldn't stop her foot from tapping impatiently.

She sneaked a peek at Alex. The tuxedo made Alex look fabulous, like a fair-haired James Bond. Catching her eye, he smiled at her. Her heart raced. She dropped one hand behind the concealing bouquet to caress her stomach, blossoming with his child.

She smiled back. Lately, Alex had been unusually gentle with her, and she welcomed the change. She hated his chilly Chandler persona. Besides, his parents were here, and Dena didn't know if she could get through the reception in the presence of three ice-cold Popsicle people.

"I do," said the groom.

"I do," breathed the bride.

Dena slipped her shoes back on, repressing a groan. Her toes had cramped from standing so long during the ceremony. She took Alex's arm and let him lead her down the aisle, following the maid of honor and the best man. How could she escape this misery? She couldn't stand in a receiving line in these heels.

Forty minutes later, Alex glanced down at Dena. She stood beside him in the receiving line with a smile seemingly frozen in place. As the last wedding guest passed them on the way to the reception, she suddenly appeared to shorten by at least two inches.

"Are you all right?" He'd read volumes about pregnancy, and he thought he knew what to expect. Spontaneous shrinkage wasn't on the list.

"Fine," she said, "now that I've taken these shoes off."

"You can't go around in just your stockings."

"I'm not even wearing stockings. I'm too hot. I can't

put these heels back on, Alex. My feet feel like boiled lobsters.''

"Do you want to go lie down for a few minutes? Should I take you home?"

Dena gave him a serene smile. ''Calm down. I'll be fine. Can you put these in the car?'' Leaning over, she picked up a pair of shoes with outlandishly high, narrow heels. She handed them to him along with her bouquet.

He let the sandals dangle from his fingers by their back straps.

Greg, nearby, let out a crack of laughter. ''They're you, Chandler.''

"I think you're right.'' Grinning, Alex swung the shoes back and forth.

"Take this, too, would you, Alex?'' Dena slipped off her bolero jacket and handed it to him before wandering toward the food.

Abandoned, Alex found a glass of champagne. He took it with him when he went to his car.

On reentering the crowded, noisy reception, he heard a band playing dance and show tunes. Some brave couples had started to twirl around the floor. In front of a group of round tables set for dinner, he saw his parents chatting with Sharyn and Martin Desmond, Blanche's parents. Alex had known the Desmonds since childhood. They were a part of the stuffy society of old-moneyed San Franciscans with whom his parents mixed.

With an inner sigh, he approached. He'd greet them before beating a retreat to enjoy the party.

"Do you think she's pregnant *again?*'' Patricia wondered aloud.

Alex stopped. If he'd had a dog's floppy ears, they'd have pricked to attention.

Martin harrumphed. ''She's already got two fatherless

children. Digging in dirt can't pay much. If she has another she'll have to go on welfare.''

Alex went rigid with anger before his sense of humor
asserted itself. The champagne was taking effect, making
him feel a little reckless and daring.

''I'm certain she's showing.'' Sharyn craned her head
to blatantly stare at Dena, who stood nearby, talking with
the maid of honor.

The two women stood in front of a bank of greenery
and roses that had been brought in to decorate the otherwise stark room. Evidently responding to a joke or
quip, Dena threw her head back and laughed uproari-
ously. The elegant line of her throat was silhouetted
against the dark foliage. Her hair glinted in the light.
Her radiance made his body tighten with desire.

Sharyn and Patricia shuddered. ''So gauche,'' Patricia
murmured.

Alex moved toward Dena. ''Hey, honey.'' He put his
arm around her shoulders and smiled at the maid of
honor. ''Excuse us.'' He stroked Dena's satiny skin,
finding her irresistible. ''Dance, baby?''

Her eyes widened as he swung her into the throng of
dancers on the floor. ''Don't step on my feet,'' she said
nervously. ''I'm not wearing shoes, remember?''

''You don't seem to have much confidence in me.''
He snuggled her closer, turning her so he could scan the
room. He covertly observed his parents, who seemed
beyond startled. His mother clutched his father's elbow,
staggering. Alex couldn't help giving Patricia a grin and
a wink. Yes, Mom definitely needed to get shaken up
once in a while.

He slipped his arms around Dena and drew her closer.
Her breasts pressed, delightfully soft, against his chest.
Oh, yeah.

"Alex, what is this about?" Dena's narrowed eyes exuded distrust.

"I'm dancing with the most beautiful woman at this wedding, the mother of my child, and you're suspicious of my motives?" He gave her his most dazzling smile, the one that Tamara always said knocked her over.

"What's going on?"

He leaned over to brush his lips against the crown of her head, enjoying the scent of the rose she'd tucked into her French twist. "I think it's time to reveal the truth to my parents, hmm?"

"This is how you've decided to do it?" A look of blank astonishment passed over her face before she relaxed and started to giggle. "Okay, they're *your* parents. Wanna give 'em an eyeful?"

He grinned. "Sure, why not?"

She cuddled closer as the band segued into a slower melody, a tune that called for cheek-to-cheek dancing. Dena's green gaze caught and held his.

His mood changed. He no longer wanted to tease his parents by pretending intimacy with her, but he wanted…what did he want? The real thing?

He wasn't sure, but her fragrance intoxicated him more than champagne. She drew closer still, flirting with her glance, using her lush body to taunt and tempt.

The lighting dimmed and Alex bent his head toward Dena's. She must have known he sought her mouth, for she lifted her chin to meet his kiss. He touched his lips to hers, keeping his eyes open to watch her reaction.

Dena closed her eyes to better savor this joy. She tasted champagne, tart and enticing, on his mouth as he opened to her. She lightly sucked on his tongue while searching through her memory. When had she last shared a French kiss? Before Steve had left, she was sure.

Then everything else receded and there was only Alex, Alex whose strong arms held her close to his perfect body. Alex, whose mouth explored hers with tenderness and skill.

Her breasts, rubbing against his chest, tingled with unslaked desire. Lust sparked into a need that spread, hot and sweet, through her entire being. She clasped his broad shoulders, shuddering with want. It had been so long…too long.

She stifled a moan as she remembered that, for Alex, this wasn't real. He was using her only to make a statement to his parents, possibly because he lacked the guts to tell them straight out that she was pregnant with his child, and Tamara's.

She opened her eyes and winked at him. His brows rose.

"You owe me for this, Chandler," she whispered.

Dena took Alex's full lower lip between her teeth. She nibbled gently, delicately, watching his blue eyes darken to midnight. His grip tightened and he suddenly whirled her through the open doors to a hall, then outside to a paved walkway.

The dark path ran alongside an artificial lake. A flood-lit fountain splashed on one side of the water. Otherwise, the shore was quiet; no one else took advantage of the romantic setting.

The warm July air slid over her naked shoulders like a lover's touch. Alex dug one hand into her hair, loosening it from its carefully contrived twist. He spread it out, and she quivered with pleasure at the sweep of hair caressing her bare skin.

This has gone too far, she realized.

Chapter Eight

Dena cleared her throat. "Well, I guess we made quite a statement back there, didn't we?"

Startled, Alex jerked away from her as reality intruded. He'd been drunk, drunk with champagne and her kisses. *I have to stop this right now,* he thought. Something about Dena threatened his control. The earthy wildness in her called to a want in his soul, a flame he didn't understand that wanted to burn free. What would happen if he let that ember flare into life?

He adjusted his cuffs while collecting himself. "Yes, but what statement was it? They probably think you're carrying my baby."

"But I am." She finger-combed her hair over her shoulders. Hairpins fell out of the updo to the ground, followed by the rose.

He picked up the flower and handed it to her. "Yes, but you're the surrogate. This is Tamara's baby." *Remember that, Chandler.*

"What do you think will shock them more, Alex?

That I'm carrying your baby, or that the child is Tami's?'' Dena tucked the bud into her bodice.

He couldn't help staring. ''It doesn't matter. Let's go. Time to deliver the news.''

Dena giggled. ''I feel like a paperboy.''

Alex glanced down at her as they walked back into the building. He didn't resist the impulse to peek down her alluring cleavage, now adorned by the pink rose. ''Millions of men wish their paperboy looked like you.'' *Quit flirting with her, Chandler. You're not supposed to flirt with the surrogate mother of your baby.*

''Thank you,'' she said primly. ''By the way, what exactly are we going to tell your parents?''

He hoped that his devil-may-care grin would hide his uncertainty. ''The truth, of course. That you're expecting their grandchild by Tamara.''

''Oh, great,'' she muttered.

They entered the ballroom with Alex towing her by the hand. Waiters circulated, passing drinks and hors d'oeuvres. Dena's tight grip showed her tension, and Alex didn't feel so wonderful himself. The glow from the champagne had faded, leaving a strong sense of purpose that drove him onward.

He steered Dena over to the little knot of people that included his parents. Dena's mother, Irina Cohen, had catered the event and was chatting with the original four gossips.

''Mom, Dad,'' he greeted them. ''Hi, Irina. Dena, have you met Blanche's parents, Sharyn and Martin Desmond?''

Dena inclined her head. The regal gesture was spoiled by her disheveled, sexy hair. ''Congratulations. Blanche is marrying a wonderful guy.''

''Thank you.'' Sharyn pointedly let her gaze drop to

Dena's midsection. "Will we be congratulating you and Alex soon?" Her eyes gleamed with malice.

Dena smiled, radiating serenity. "I certainly hope so. We expect our happy event to take place early next January."

Alex mentally applauded her composure.

His mother's mouth gaped like a surprised grouper's. "The two of you ought to be ashamed of yourselves, cavorting in public with dear Tamara still warm in her grave." She glared at him.

Irina adjusted the jacket of her tuxedo-style pantsuit. "I have a feeling my dahlink Tamara planned everything that's happened."

Leighton choked on his Scotch. "You mean to say that Tamara wanted her sister and her husband to— to—" Alex's father gestured at Dena's belly with the cut-crystal tumbler, half-full of dark amber liquid.

"To have a baby?" Irina asked. "You can say it, Leighton. We're all adults here."

Alex decided that he didn't want the situation to spiral out of control. Nor did he want inaccurate rumors started. "Irina's right. Tamara asked Dena to carry our child to term."

Patricia dropped her champagne flute. It broke on the floor, splashing glass shards and wine on her husband's feet. Sharyn gasped. Martin started to laugh. A waiter rushed over to clean up the mess, towel in hand.

"Patricia, for Pete's sake. You dumped booze in my shoes!" Leighton snapped. He stepped away from the waiter.

Patricia ignored him. "'Our child.' What do you mean?"

"Dena is the surrogate mother of Tamara's and my baby."

Dena smiled. "And very happy to be of service."

Martin laughed harder. Between guffaws, he gasped, "I've gotta hand it to you. You sure know how to be outrageous." He ogled Dena with obvious admiration.

Alex shot him a long, cool glance intended to quell, and noticed Dena's lips pressed together into a pencil-thin line.

Patricia's breathing grew ragged. She grabbed his father's elbow. "Leighton! Do something!"

"What do you expect me to do, Patty?" Shaking her off, Leighton sucked down some more Scotch. "Lord, but we live in a crazy world. Nothing good can come out of something—of something so bizarre and unnatural."

"I, for one, think it's wonderful. I look forward to welcoming *our* new grandchild into the world come New Year's." Irina gave Alex's parents a glare through narrowed eyes, as though to say, *Act happy about this, you morons!*

Patricia and Leighton looked bewildered. "Alex, why didn't you tell us about this before?" his mother asked.

"We wanted to wait until we were sure the pregnancy was progressing normally," Alex said. "I didn't want to get your hopes up about a grandchild unless we were sure. A lot of things could still go wrong."

"Really?" Patricia sounded almost hopeful.

Dena and Irina glowered at Patricia, their two sets of cold green eyes lit with a baleful glow. Alex had never before noted the similarities between tall, voluptuous Dena and her petite mother. Now both redheads reflected the same temper about to explode. Alex figured he'd better defuse the situation, fast.

"Mom, Dad, I know you've had a little bit of a shock." He cursed himself, belatedly realizing he should have broken the news in a conventional manner to his conventional parents. Now he'd have to struggle to calm his mother.

He took Patricia's arm and led her to a seat. His father followed. Alex sat in another chair close to hers. "Mom, this baby was very important to Tami, and it's important to me, too."

Patricia pushed a strand of hair out of her eyes, her hand shaking. "I know that, son. I remember how Tamara drove herself into the grave with her desire for a child."

"One thing had nothing to do with the other." Alex's voice rose with fury.

"I didn't mean that," Patricia protested tearfully. "But she would have been a much happier person if she could have reconciled herself to childlessness."

"Are you saying that I should give up, too?" Alex stood.

Suddenly, Dena was there, pressing a calming hand onto his shoulder. "Alex, sit back down. Leighton, Patricia, this baby is real." She rubbed her stomach. "You can either be happy about it or make Alex miserable. You choose."

Alex's father took a deep breath. "Since you put it that way…" He glanced at Patricia.

She sighed. "I don't want to be someone's old grandma."

"Oh, come now," Alex said, injecting a note of heartiness into his tone. "You can be the first to show off photos of your grandchild. You'll be the envy of all your friends."

Patricia sighed again.

Crisis averted, the wedding dinner proceeded without incident. Alex sat tucking away cake when Dena said,

"Oh, no. The bouquet toss." She scrunched down in her chair, as though trying to make herself tiny and invisible.

"Come along, Dena!" Blanche shrilled. She'd been hitting the champagne and sounded a little tipsy to Alex.

"That's okay. I've already been married. It's only fair to let others get a chance." Dena arched her brows. "I'd be nuts to marry again after what happened the first time."

Alex smiled but couldn't help wondering if she'd ever change her mind.

A crowd of single females jammed the center of the dance floor, just in front of the table where Dena and Alex sat. A waiter passed by and offered coffee.

"If it's decaf." Dena extended her cup.

"No caffeine?" Alex asked. "I'm impressed. You're very careful."

She nodded solemnly. "You betcha. Not only is it bad for the baby, but when this little nipper gets bigger, it'll keep him awake, just like anyone else. Can you imagine a kicking kid keeping you up all night?" She shuddered, then sipped her coffee.

"One! Two! Three! Go!" the women chanted.

Alex watched as Blanche flung the bouquet high over her shoulder. It sailed through the air in a steep arc. Hitting the edge of a light fixture, it changed trajectory.

The flowers fell out of the air and onto Dena's dessert plate. She coughed, then slammed her coffee cup down, gasping for air.

As Alex whacked Dena on her back, he caught a glimpse of his mother's face. Patricia looked as though she was going to have a stroke.

Alex took Dena home long past midnight. She stumbled out of the Jag on her bare feet, picking her way across the rough surface of the driveway past the baby-sitter's VW bug. He grabbed Dena's arm to help her onto the porch and into the cozy depths of the rattan couch.

''Oof!'' Dena let herself relax into the soft cushions.

Alex sat next to her. ''How are your feet?''

Stretching them out in front of her, she wiggled her toes. ''Better than if I'd kept those sandals on. Whatever possessed Blanche to order them?''

''She must have thought they looked good, but I saw a lot of barefoot girls tonight. Did anyone wear them all evening?''

''Beats me.'' She leaned back with a sigh.

Moonlight flashed off something glittering on her toes. ''Dena, what's on your feet?''

Turning, she planted one foot onto his thigh. Even in the dim light, little luminescent designs painted onto her toes gleamed. ''What are these?'' He lifted her foot and bent forward to get a better view.

''Blanche told me in advance that she was decorating the hall with pink roses, so I had roses painted onto my toenails. Neat, huh?''

He laughed. ''They're the most absurd things I ever saw.'' He scrabbled his fingers across her sensitive arch.

''Hey, you promised, no tickling!''

''Yeah, I did, didn't I?'' He massaged the ball of her foot until she groaned with pleasure, then stroked her ankle. ''Hey, I bet your feet could use a massage.''

''Umm, all that standing. But I had fun.'' She sighed happily when he transferred his attention to her heel. ''This is really sweet of you, Alex.''

''You deserve a little pampering.'' He continued the foot massage, caressing each toe. ''Tamara loved this, too. I often rubbed her feet after a party. She didn't like high heels, either.''

''No one does, but a lot of women wear them. Crazy, huh?'' She adjusted her weight against the side arm of the couch.

''Hey, Dena, you were wonderful tonight.'' He'd learned the answer to one of his questions about her. She could hold her own in any group, on any occasion, with ease. As long as she didn't have to wear stiletto heels.

''Me?'' She gave a sleepy chuckle. ''I didn't do anything.''

''You were perfect.'' He reached for her other foot. Dena had sexy feet, with high, elegant arches. What would she do if he nibbled on her big toe? Stifling his naughty urge, he went to work on her heel and arches.

She stretched, appearing to relax a little bit more. Her other foot stirred in his lap.

The flesh at his groin hardened. He couldn't deceive himself any longer, not after that kiss. He wanted her badly. *Steady, Chandler,* he told himself. *She's not your woman. And she probably never will be.*

If Dena wouldn't marry, would she take a lover? Had she, since Steve had left? Alex had never heard that she had a boyfriend, but he'd been so wrapped up in Tamara that he wouldn't have noticed.

Dena was a beautiful, sensual woman. Alex couldn't ignore the way men looked at her, with blatant lust in their eyes. Everything about her screamed sex. Her lush red hair reminded him of long, sweaty summer nights rumpling the sheets. Her voluptuous body had abundant breasts, breasts that would nurture his child. He longed to bury his face in the fragrant cave between those splendid mounds.

The moonlight painted the curve of her cheekbone with silver. Her full lips, slightly open, emitted a snore.

Alex stifled a laugh. She wasn't perfect, after all. Lifting her feet off his lap, he slid carefully off the couch and settled her heels back onto a cushion. In late July, with such warm weather, sleeping on the screened porch wouldn't hurt Dena. In fact, the veranda seemed more pleasant than the cramped, stuffy condo where he lived.

Dena awakened to hear the quiet hum of a well-tuned car motor. Sitting up, she saw Alex's Jag depart. She stretched her arms above her head and grimaced as the underwired bustier dug into her side.

What had happened? Had she actually fallen asleep during the foot massage? *He'll think I find him boring.* Nothing could be further from the truth, but the foot massage had made her feel so cherished and relaxed that she'd slipped into slumber.

She'd dreamed of Alex's kiss on the dance floor. He'd tasted so good. She felt so complete in his arms, as though the missing piece in the puzzle of her life had fallen into place. If they'd kept it up they would have made a baby the old-fashioned way, she realized with a sleepy chuckle.

She went into her house. Rachel, her baby-sitter, napped on the sofa in the living room. A music video, the sound muted, occupied the TV screen. Dena decided not to wake her. A college student, Rachel needed her rest. It was okay if she spent the night.

Mounting the stairs, Dena wondered whether Alex caused the elation she'd felt during the kiss, or if she would have known the same bliss in the arms of another man. Maybe after the baby was born she should get out a little more. She'd shoved her desires onto the back burner when Steve walked and the twins were born. Jack and Miri had dominated her life for more than four years.

She peeked into Miriam's bedroom. Only a fluff of her daughter's dark hair could be seen from beneath her Disney sheets. Across the hall, Jack slept in a tangled mess, one arm flung wide. He'd tossed his stuffed bear across the room.

Dena smiled. She didn't regret a single sacrifice made for her twins. They were special children. She treasured every precious moment.

In her room, she stripped off the ridiculous gown. She couldn't believe she'd worn a butt bow. She dropped the uncomfortable bustier on top of the dress and went to her bathroom to wash off her makeup.

She examined her reflection in the mirror. She used sunscreen daily, so she tanned but didn't wrinkle. Did Alex like the tiny laugh lines next to her eyes? She squelched the thought. *He probably never noticed them.*

All in all, she still looked pretty good, considering what she'd been through during the past five years. She'd worked hard to achieve balance in her life. With the twins a little older, maybe she could have some fun…after the baby was born.

She slipped between the sheets. As she clutched the pillow to her breast, her body cried out for Alex's arms to hold her tight.

He's only being nice to you because of the baby, she reminded herself. *Don't be fooled!*

Chapter Nine

Alex sucked in a breath of the hot, humid air. The sultry August afternoon presaged a thunderstorm. Stepping to Dena's door, he tapped on the stained glass pane, wondering how she'd respond to his gift. She could be so unpredictable. That quality had increased with her girth, hormones flooding her body with complex emotions he couldn't unravel.

The door flew open, revealing Irina. She kissed him hurriedly on the cheek. "We have to hurry, we're late." She turned. "Dena! We're late!"

"We?" Alex asked as he walked into the entry.

"Alex, dahlink, I have a favor to ask. May I take Dena to the ultrasound today? I really want to see the baby." Irina's eyes beseeched.

Alex hesitated. He liked to see his child stir in Dena's womb. But Irina was already the most involved grandmother this baby would have. "Sure."

"Can you watch the twins?"

He hesitated again, the memory of the zoo incident,

and others, fresh in his mind. But they'd taken place years before. Jack and Miri were older, smarter and more cooperative. They'd been fine on Mother's Day, hadn't they?

"They're napping," Irina said. "Please, Alex. I'm sure they won't be any trouble."

Alex relaxed. How many problems could two sleeping children cause? "All right."

"Oh, thanks so much." Irina stood on her toes to kiss Alex on the cheek.

He leaned over to help her reach her target. "No problem." He walked into the living room as Dena came down the stairs.

A loose summer dress of blue chambray belled attractively over her stomach. The sloppy, sexy twist of hair had slipped from its perch atop her head, allowing red-gold locks to frame her suntanned face. Cute little freckles dotted her straight nose.

"Dena." He caressed her stomach while sneaking a hug and a peck to her cheek. Maybe he'd get a real kiss when she saw what he'd bought for her. "What's he doing?"

She smiled and moved his hand to one side of her belly.

The baby kicked, making Alex laugh. "There's nothing like this feeling, is there?"

"No, there isn't." She curved a hand around herself. "Is it okay if Mom comes with me today?"

He nodded.

"Oh, that's wonderful. Listen. The kids are asleep and should stay that way until we get back. But if they wake up, give them a snack. There's juice and carrot sticks in the fridge." She grabbed her purse on the way to the door where Irina waited, purse in hand.

Her hand on the knob, Dena turned. "And Alex, in case you haven't eaten lunch, I made you some egg salad. Bye!" She left.

Alone, Alex said aloud, "She made me egg salad. Hmm." Tamara had been an ace in the kitchen, but her on-the-go life didn't allow her to fix workday lunches. His mother would have told the cook to take care of his hunger. No one had ever made him egg salad. He was doubly glad he'd gone to the trouble of—

"Alex!" Dena's eyes glinted as she barreled through the doorway. She grabbed his arm. "Alex, what is this?" She pointed out the door where an oversize, yellow pickup dominated the driveway. Blocked in next to it, Dena's old clunker looked like a forlorn wreck.

He grinned. She wasn't so unpredictable, after all. He dangled a key in front of her nose. "'This' is your new truck. 'This' is its key."

Her mouth dropped open. "Uh, bu—but—"

"It's not often that I steal the words right out of your mouth."

She recovered herself. "Alex, this is very nice, I suppose, but I really don't need you to buy me a truck."

"I didn't buy you anything. Tamara did." *Just one little white lie won't hurt,* Alex told himself. "She left a lot of money for the support of the baby. I decided that I don't want my unborn child riding around in your old truck."

"I *like* my old truck." Dena's face became a furious red. "I'm used to my old truck."

"Try to see reason, Dena. There's no tread left on your tires. I checked last week. You're going to have to replace the transmission and the muffler. Worse, there isn't enough room in that junk heap for you and the twins."

"I don't need this, Alex. I don't need you to run my life."

"Won't you at least take it for a drive and check it out?" Tucking her arm into his elbow, he dragged her unwilling weight across the porch toward the truck.

Irina had already climbed inside. "Dahlink, this is terrific. It has a back seat for the twins and everything." She stuck her head out the window. "It must have at least ten cup-holders."

Dena rolled her eyes. "Cup-holders. The way to my mother's heart is through the cup-holders." She looked at the new truck, then back at her elderly rust bucket. She sighed. "Okay, Alex, you win. What's the insurance gonna cost me?"

He waved a hand. "You don't have to worry about the insurance or the registration. It's for the support of the baby, you see."

Dena accelerated onto Fair Oaks Boulevard, with grudging admiration at the truck's smooth handling. "You know, Mom, I think Alex has been acting kinda, well, weird." Her thoughts were in turmoil because of Alex Chandler—again.

"What's to dislike? He's behaving like a man. He's taking care of you and the baby."

"I don't need him to take care of me," Dena grumbled.

"With Steve gone, someone has to."

"I've tried hard to take care of myself."

"You've done a good job, but I'm glad he's around. I don't have to be the only one to worry about my daughter."

Guilt tinged Dena's moodiness. "Oh, Mom, I know that since Steve left you've had to help out a lot."

"Dahlink, you know it's not the money." Her mother started to play with the radio. "I haven't had to contribute to your household for a year or two. You've proven to everyone that you can make it on your own. So now you can accept a helping hand, without shame."

"I guess. But this is more than a helping hand. This is a really expensive gift. This is Alex trying to take over my life…again." Dena recalled her dependence upon Steve. *Remember what happened with that relationship,* she admonished herself. *Don't get caught in that trap again!*

"Learn how to be pampered. For your old mother, it's a relief knowing that there's someone else in your life who's capable and who cares about you. A lot."

"Do you think he really cares?" Dena drove over a bridge and merged with traffic onto J Street. She didn't want to take the truck. Somehow, acceptance of this gift would be tantamount to accepting Alex's central role in her life. She didn't know if she was ready to let a man back into her world. "He said he got the truck for the baby."

"In a pig's eye."

Another of Mom's folksy sayings. "Huh? Every time he does something nice, he tells me it's for the baby." Dena recalled Alex's kisses at the wedding. Lust, a bright, unquenchable flame, flared deep inside. She squirmed in her seat.

"Mark my words. There's something more going on than simple concern for the baby. The twins tell me Alex is around your house almost every day."

"Yeah, checking up on me, my diet, even my tire tread…I feel as though he doesn't trust me."

"Those are just excuses. He wants to see you. What

was that scene at Greg and Blanche's wedding about, hmm?''

Dena shrugged, hoping she hid the fire within her. ''That was his cutesy way of announcing to his parents that we're having his baby.'' Boy, that sounded strange. Maybe Alex did have an ulterior motive.

''Nonsense. Alex could have phoned, written a letter or simply told them. He kissed you because he wanted to, no matter what he says or what he tells himself.''

Left alone, Alex took off his jacket and loosened his tie. Warm satisfaction pervaded him. He knew that if he got Dena to drive the truck, she'd keep it. More a luxury vehicle than a pickup, it handled like a dream.

He liked making life easier for her. He'd hated to watch Dena struggling with her old truck. It was extra stress she—and the baby, of course—didn't need.

Alex made himself comfortable with egg salad and the *Wall Street Journal* at Dena's kitchen table. An hour later, he lifted his head from an article about Asian stock options, sure he'd heard a thump from upstairs. Standing, he stretched, then cocked an ear to listen. Silence. Perhaps he'd imagined the sound.

No. He heard the faint chatter of high, childish voices. He smiled. The twins were awake.

He trotted upstairs to find…nothing. No kids. But in Jack's empty bedroom, he could see evidence of recent occupancy: a messy bed with rumpled sheets. Toys and books on the floor.

He turned into Miriam's room and stopped short, his way to her unoccupied bed blocked by a kid's plastic table. Surrounded by four chairs, it was set up for a mad tea party, place cards, teapot, and all.

Intrigued, Alex looked closer. In front of a giant

stuffed bear was a place card written in awkward green letters: *Jack*. The chair occupied by Minnie Mouse had a card that read *Miriam*. Barbie also sat at the table. *Mom*.

Big Bird's effigy was named *Alex*.

Alex's breath rushed out of his lungs. He stared at the toy family clustered around the table. The realization that the twins saw him as part of their family floored him. His breath shortened. His heart contracted as something twisted in his chest.

This was everything he wanted.

How could he make this dream come true?

Then, another thump came, this time from outside the room, but…above? Stepping into the hall, Alex stared upward toward the mysterious sounds that surely marked the twins' location. The attic? How had they gotten up there?

He opened the door of the guest room to see a ladder leading to a square hole in the ceiling. Aha. The twins had gone exploring Dena's attic.

"Jack! Miri!" He didn't know what was up there. What if one of them got hurt?

Happy screeches greeted his call. "Unka Alex!" Miriam tumbled down the ladder into his arms. Smudges decorated her nose and cheek. Her T-shirt and shorts were grubby, as usual. The twins attracted dirt the way a magnet drew iron filings.

"Hi, sweetheart." He gave her a big squeeze. He'd get his shirt cleaned.

"Where's Mommy?" Jack stuck his head through the hole in the ceiling.

"She went to the doctor with Grandma. Come on down, you scamp." Putting Miriam down, Alex extended an arm to his nephew.

"Help me, Uncle Alex." Jack disappeared. A few seconds later, Alex could hear scraping sounds from the attic.

"Jack, what are you doing?"

"Come up here so you can see." A sly note had entered Jack's voice.

"Plee-eeze, Unka Alex?" Miriam tugged at his pant leg. "Plee-eeze help us?"

"Sure. Help with what?" Alex asked, belatedly realizing he'd committed himself without getting the facts first.

Miriam clambered up the ladder. "We're gonna help Mommy. We wanna set up the baby's room."

Uh-oh. He was walking on dangerous ground. "What did Mommy tell you about the baby, sweetie?" He climbed up the ladder and peered into the attic. Crowded with boxes and furniture, it was dim, hot and dusty. He could vaguely see the children as they tugged at a rectangular, wooden object. He came closer. A crib.

"Hey, kids, wait." Alex sat down on a stack of boxes labeled Books, in large red lettering. "Come on over here."

Jack climbed into Alex's lap. Miriam leaned against his side, and he slipped an arm around her.

"What has Mommy told you about the baby?"

"That it's your baby and won't really be our little brother or sister." Jack sounded unhappy.

A frown crinkled Miriam's face. "But that isn't right. Mommies and daddies make babies together, don't they? And our daddy's gone. Did you give Mommy her baby?"

Alex's stomach dropped to his toes. He gulped. "It's Auntie Tami's baby, and mine."

Two little faces, filled with bewilderment, stared at him.

"That can't be. Auntie Tami's in heaven with the angels. Mommy said so." Jack pulled away from Alex's hug. He returned to the crib, trying to drag it closer to the attic ladder.

"And it's in Mommy's tummy. That makes it her baby." Her lip trembling, Miriam left Alex's side and helped Jack.

Both twins seemed hopelessly confused, and Alex wasn't sure any explanation could help. As far as the twins were concerned, Auntie Tami was in heaven and angels didn't bear children.

He sighed. "Please trust me on this."

The twins exchanged glances, then tried to shove the crib down the attic ladder.

"Hey!" Alex grabbed the crib. "Wait a minute!"

"Will you take it down for us, Unka Alex?" Miriam asked. "The baby will need a place to sleep."

Alex knelt beside his little niece and took her into his arms. "The baby will be living with me. He's—he's my baby."

Her eyes filled. "No-o-o-o!"

He hugged her tight.

"But what about Mommy's milkies?" Jack asked. "Mommy said that the baby will need to drink from them to get strong, just like we did."

Mommy's milkies. He'd rather have a root canal without anesthesia than continue this conversation.

He drew a deep breath. "You're right, Jack. The baby will have to live with Mommy until—until—for a while."

"Yay!" Both children screamed high and loud enough to shatter windows a mile away.

"Now, let's get this crib downstairs," he said.

Dena walked in while Alex struggled to fit the changing table into the closet. The twins had run downstairs when their grandmother arrived. "Alex, what are you doing?"

"I'm putting this into the closet, to save space."

"Good idea, I guess." She looked closer. "What is it?"

"The baby's changing table." Task completed, he eased out of the closet and scrutinized her belly. "How did it go?"

"Fine. We're perfect." She patted her stomach.

"And the truck?"

She huffed. "Alex, you mustn't do things like that again."

"Are you going to keep the truck?"

"I love the truck. Thank you." She leaned toward him and deposited a quick, shy kiss on his cheek.

"You're—you're welcome." Though swift as the flutter of a hummingbird's wing, the kiss delighted him more than anything since Tamara's death. Except for maybe that kiss at the wedding—whew! His heart rate leaped at the memory.

"But you're turning my life upside down, you know that? And what are you doing to my guest room?" Her voice turned matter-of-fact, calming him down a degree or two.

"The twins persuaded me that the baby should live here after it's born."

"What?" A slight smile played over her lips. "Alex, you've emphasized that this isn't my baby."

"How are you going to breast-feed if the baby isn't with you?" His glance strayed to her breasts. Heaven help him.

"How are you going to become a parent if your baby isn't with *you?*"

He hesitated. "It's not for forever. Look, the twins don't understand what's going on. They seemed so happy when I said I'd set up the room. I just couldn't tell them no."

She frowned, crossing her arms over her chest. "Parenthood means having to say no sometimes, Alex."

"But right now, they can't accept that this is my baby, Tamara's and mine. At some point, they'll understand, and then I'll take him home."

"Maybe you're right." She sat on the edge of the bed. "They'll either get bored or jealous of the new baby, I bet. Then he can move out." She beamed at him. "Good thinking."

Alex couldn't help feeling proud. Fatherhood wasn't hard. He'd already arranged for his child's first accommodations and even set up his room.

She continued, "But the twins may miss the baby after he's gone."

"Oh, we'll visit often," Alex promised, feeling generous. "We'll come over all the time. I want my baby to be best friends with his cousins."

"The only problem is that I can't handle two young children and the baby as well. Have you thought about a nanny?"

Alex froze. A nanny? A stranger care for his baby? "No."

"Then who's going to do it?" She sounded irritatingly reasonable. "Mom works and so do I. So do you. I'll probably take some time off, but after that, what?"

Alex checked out the bed upon which Dena sat. The double bed was smaller than the king-size he preferred, but he could rough it—for his baby. An image of the kids' tea table, set for four, flashed through his mind.

He faltered, then gathered his courage. "I have no right to ask, but can I stay here?"

Her eyes opened wide. "Uh, uh, I guess." She took a deep breath, swelling her chest. "It would solve the problem, wouldn't it?"

He tried not to ogle her breasts. "I…I suppose I'll have to take some time off from work until the baby is old enough to go into day care, but I don't want to do that until he's really big."

"Really big?" she asked, with mockery slightly edging her tone. She leaned back onto the mattress, letting her elbows support her weight. The position drew her dress tightly across her bosom.

Really big. Oh, God.

His temperature escalated, leaving his mouth dry and his pulse pounding as if he'd run a marathon. "Well, uh, I haven't decided when, exactly. I'll wait until he's born, and then we can see how he grows. Aren't all children different?"

"Can't argue with that." Her green eyes twinkled with a teasing glint. How was he going to live with a flirting, teasing Dena without wanting her?

Answer: he couldn't. Living in the big house at the end of Shadownook would be either heaven or hell…he didn't know which. But he'd find out in a few short months.

"Isn't it time to talk about what you'll call the baby, instead of 'him,' and 'it?'"

"Oh, no. Tamara and I discussed this at length. She wanted to wait and see what the baby was like. We talked about a couple of names, but decided not to pick one until we met the baby."

Dena grinned. "One doesn't exactly meet a baby." She caressed her belly. "I feel as though we've already met, and know each other quite well."

"Really?" He sat on the bed beside her, dangerously close to her tempting warmth, her flowery scent. "And what do you know about the baby?"

"For one thing, he's a night owl."

"Oh, no." Alex groaned. "I'm a morning person."

Dena grinned. "He likes to dance the rumba at midnight."

"Great."

They both laughed. Alex, mesmerized by her emerald eyes, shimmering with humor, couldn't resist slipping an arm around her waist.

She turned to him, looking startled. He dropped his hand. "Uh, by the way, Alex, Mom and I drove by your office on the way home."

"Why? It's not on the most direct route."

"I was just driving the truck around. It really handles nicely."

"Good." He'd known she couldn't resist as long as he got her behind the wheel.

"I wanted to show Mom one of the buildings I'm landscaping on C Street, a few blocks from yours. Listen, I could do wonderful things with your office. Can you talk to Greg about freeing up some funds? I could really make it a showplace."

He groaned. "That old house is nothing but a black hole that sucks up money."

"It's gorgeous. In five years, you'll be glad that you and Greg bought it. Those renovated Victorians are worth a fortune. But you have to put some money into your investment to make it worthwhile."

Standing, he paced the floor. "All right. Write up

some plans and the three of us can meet about it. But don't work too hard. Aren't you supposed to be cutting back on your schedule?''

She shrugged. "I don't see why."

"We have to start Lamaze soon and I want you to work fewer hours come October.''

"If you felt that way, why did you get me a new truck?''

"I know you need a pickup now. I'm talking about later.''

"Alex, please don't tell me what to do.'' She stood. "Quit rearranging my life, okay?''

"IVF babies are frequently premature. Listen, I know what I'm talking about.''

"I feel great and Dr. Mujedin thinks we're doing fine.'' She patted her stomach. "Don't worry. If I feel anything weird, I promise I'll cut back. But I'm a healthy twenty-eight-year-old woman. I could have a dozen kids if I wanted.''

He turned away. "That's what Tami thought.''

"Hey,'' she said gently, touching his shoulders. "There's nothing to be scared about.''

"I'm not scared.'' But his voice came out too loudly.

She continued to rub his shoulders. Her hands felt good, too good, before she dug a finger into a tight muscle. Grimacing, he jerked away.

"You need to relax. Stay for dinner?'' She lightened her touch into a caress.

He looked over his shoulder. He couldn't interpret the expression on Dena's face. At the least suggestion he'd kiss her. Her wide eyes were filled with—what? Pity? Tenderness?

He wanted her, but wasn't into a pity party. He'd better put the brakes on whatever was happening between them. "What's on the menu?"

She raised a brow and let her hands drop. "Whatever Mom wants to cook."

"Irina's cooking?" He tried to sound casual. "I'll call Greg and tell him not to expect me back for the rest of the afternoon."

"Glad the cook interests you." Disappointment knifing her gut, Dena left the baby's room. She went down the stairs and out the back door without a word to anyone. She walked across the lawn to the stone bench set by her little pond and sank onto it. She waited quietly, watching the still surface of the water, letting her thoughts calm.

Alex could throw her into a tailspin in the wink of an eye. She couldn't figure him out. When he'd been married to Tamara, he'd seemed like the dullest, drabbest man alive, the ultimate accountant, as mundane as mud.

But today, he'd bought her a truck, rearranged her house and wangled an invitation to stay with her for an unspecified period of time. On top of that, he'd touched her heart, invited her into heaven, then slammed the door in her face.

What was going on?

When Alex said that he'd decided to let the baby live with her, she nearly let out a whoop of elation. She already loved her little niece or nephew and wanted to keep the baby close. She knew he'd get a better start in life if he stayed with her after his birth. She'd hesitated to ask Alex because he seemed so possessive of the baby. What had the twins said to persuade Alex to let the baby stay?

A pang of tenderness, sweetness edged with pain, stabbed her heart when she remembered his concern for the twins' feelings. Alex was so kind. How many men would care about two four-year-olds? But Alex did.

Then he said he'd live with her, and even put his arm around her before he'd inexplicably withdrawn.

The turtle poked his head out of the water, then swam to a rock. After a few minutes, the water flattened and stilled, again reflecting the cloudy sky.

Dena recalled the first time the baby furniture had been set up. Steve had been gone about two months when she and Irina had ordered cribs and a changing table from a catalog. They'd built them in the kids' rooms. Her mother had been by her side supporting her, but Dena had cried until her eyes swelled and her nose stopped up.

Alex was different, in every way. Giving where Steve had been selfish. Concerned where Steve had been thoughtless. Steve hadn't cared about the car she drove—in fact, one month he'd taken the money for her truck payment and bought a new snowboard.

Alex often confused and angered her, *but hey—nobody's perfect,* she thought. Alex's urge to control her sprang from his love for the baby. She'd wanted him to care about her, also, but she really couldn't fault him.

Much.

Alex exited the back door carrying two glasses. His shirtsleeves were rolled to the elbows and his tie was gone. She remembered seeing it on the bed in the guest room. He'd hung his jacket on a chair downstairs. She wondered what other articles of clothing Alex had left scattered around her house.

When he lived with her, no doubt he'd make his masculine presence known: raised toilet seats in the bathroom and copies of *Sports Illustrated* on the coffee table. Did she want that?

As she watched him, a frisson of pleasure ran through her. Yes, she did want that, and she wanted him, tall, handsome Alex striding across the lawn toward her with his blond hair rumpled as though she'd run her hands through it. She wanted him more than anything, and she didn't know how she'd control herself when he lived with her. Why had she agreed?

Because of the baby. For the good of the child, and that was paramount. Not only would the baby benefit, but she could teach Alex so much about parenting. From Desitin to diapering, bathing to burping, he'd learn it all. She'd make sure that Alex could take care of the baby before she had to give him up.

Letting them go after they'd lived with her, perhaps for months…she grimaced. That would be like descending into hell. How would she cope? She swallowed hard and yanked her mind away from that horrible thought.

Alex handed her a glass of lemonade. She sipped the chilled drink while covertly scrutinizing him. He looked as though he'd managed to relax, judging by his messy clothing. She reached up to test her observation, poking a finger into his rock-hard shoulder.

"Hmm," she said. "Either you're working out too much or you're still pretty uptight."

"I've been lifting weights as well as running this summer."

I wonder what he looks like naked. The thought zipped across her mind, along with the memory of him, nude to the waist, reclining on her bed. A sexual heat sizzled through her body.

He turned to face her, his eyes dark and serious. "I *am* scared, you know. You hit it on the first try."

She bit her lip. "I didn't mean to hurt you or make

you admit something you don't want to talk about.''
Finishing the lemonade, she set the glass on the ground.

"It's all right.'' He put his drink on the bench, then
took her into his embrace. "I just couldn't bear it if
anything happened to you or the baby.''

Dena struggled to maintain a cool exterior. His mood
and feelings were so obviously different from hers. She
wanted to hug him back, hold him tight, explore his
gloriously masculine body and nibble on his sexy, pouty
lower lip. But she knew that, with her swollen physique,
he couldn't possibly want to touch her in the same way
she desired him.

"Alex, you're taking such good care of me that I'm
sure nothing will happen.'' She gave him a sisterly sort
of squeeze, friendly but not too affectionate, then pulled
away. Did he look disappointed? Nah…she was dreaming.

Chapter Ten

Dena pulled off her gardening gloves and used two hands to support her lower back as she arched and stretched. Now in her sixth month, she could truly feel the weight of her baby. Turning her head, she saw Alex at the window of the renovated Victorian that housed Chandler and Holloway, Accountants. He mouthed at her, *"Are you all right?"*

She gave him a smile and a thumbs-up. After a few weeks of wrangling, she'd persuaded Greg and Alex to give her a fat budget for the complete redesign of the grounds surrounding their beautiful old building.

Dena loved her work and enjoyed making this yard come alive. She'd planned an èclectic garden with benches and a small pond, perfect for coffee breaks and outdoor lunches when the weather allowed. She'd plant annuals and bulbs every year, while camellias would provide off-season color and interest. Shaded by large magnolias the grounds allowed for the use of some striking shade-loving plants.

The October wind swirled leaves around her ankles as she walked back to her truck, donning her gloves. She gave the shiny surface of her new yellow truck a pat. *Thank you, Tami. Or Alex. Or whoever.* Dena had decided just to accept the gift and quit torturing herself with questions she couldn't answer.

Learning to trust Alex had been a big step, Dena reflected. Accepting the truck physically embodied this shift in her emotions. She'd learned that trusting a man could be…okay. She just didn't know if anything more would ever be possible.

Dena lowered the tailgate and prepared to carry a big Japanese maple to the hole she'd dug next to Alex's window. The lacy green foliage of this particular variety turned a brilliant crimson in the autumn; when the leaves dropped, the tree's unusual red branches were exposed, providing winter color. Alex would see something beautiful out of his window during every season of the year.

She put one knee on the tailgate and reached for the tree's root ball, wrapped in burlap. She tugged it forward and into her arms, remembering to bend her knees. She hoped her legs rather than her sore back would carry the weight.

She took two staggering steps over to the hole before a stabbing pain lanced through her back. Dropping the tree, she cried out. Tottering, she clutched herself as she fell to the soft lawn.

Hearing a scream, Alex looked out his window. Dena writhed on the ground. *Oh, my God. Is the baby coming?* Preemies were common among IVF babies. He knew that he should have made Dena stop working at the beginning of October, but she'd promised to avoid stress.

He found himself chanting ''Please, God, please, God,

please God'' as he dashed out of the front door of the building.

Greg followed him. "What is it?"

"I don't know. Call 911." Alex knelt on the ground next to her.

Breathing hard, she whimpered, making agonized moans. Each hit him like a stab in his gut.

"What is it? What is it?"

She gasped and appeared to control herself. "That tree. That damn tree. I threw my back out."

"Are you sure it isn't the baby?"

"Yeah, I'm sure. I'm not having contractions, not even Braxton-Hicks. It's my back." She closed her eyes. Her brow furrowed with pain.

He heaved a deep sigh of relief. "Just relax. Greg is calling for an ambulance."

Her eyes popped open. "An ambulance? Alex, don't call an ambulance for a sore back."

"I'm not taking any chances with you and the baby. I'm going to get Dr. Mujedin to meet us at the ER, just to check you over and make sure."

"Alex—" A look of utter exasperation crossed Dena's face. "Well, okay. I think you're crazy, but nothing I say is going to change what you do." She gave a delicate gasp.

"Quit talking."

"You're going to win this argument, but it's not because you're right, do you hear? It's because I don't have the strength to fight with you."

He couldn't help grinning at her sassy attitude, despite the situation. She might have been seriously hurt, and he didn't want to think about what could have happened to the baby. "Just as long as I win. Remember that, all right?" He dropped a kiss onto her sweaty forehead. "Alex gets to win."

"Ms. Randolph, you are going to have to be more careful." Dr. Mujedin rubbed his stethoscope over Dena's belly, now clad in a blue hospital gown. "I realize that you are a healthy young woman, but you cannot continue to pretend that you aren't pregnant."

Alex hovered at the door of the ER cubicle. "How's the baby?"

"The baby is fine, but Ms. Randolph must slow down."

Dena listened resentfully. Over the doctor's shoulder, she could see Alex pumping his fist into the air and doing a victory dance. She glared at him.

"Ms. Randolph?"

"Er, yes, doctor." She shifted her focus to Dr. Mujedin while silently fuming at Alex. Darn him, he'd made her act rudely to the doctor. "But I worked up until my twins were born."

"Every pregnancy is different."

Dena sighed. "What exactly do you want me to do?"

"Decrease your work hours. Exercise moderately, and avoid the hard physical labor." He smiled at her. "Start your Lamaze classes with Mr. Chandler and...pamper yourself. Enjoy this special time in your life."

The last time she'd been pregnant, she'd almost gone mad with worry over her future. Now, because of her sister's thoughtfulness, Dena had no financial stress. Dr. Mujedin was right. She could hire someone to do the backbreaking work of maintaining Dena's Gardens while she supervised.

She heaved a deep sigh and...just let go. "Sounds great."

"I'm glad we are in agreement. Mr. Chandler, I'll release Ms. Randolph to you. Take good care of her." The doctor left.

Alex picked her up from the examination table and eased her to the floor. "No more fights?"

She shook her head. She couldn't argue. Dr. Mujedin had taken away all her ammo.

"No more disputes about taking better care of yourself?"

"Nope. You gonna take me home and pamper me?" She grinned at him. Despite her sore back, her body tingled delightfully where she rubbed against him.

He embraced her, smiling. "Oh, yes. I have to make one stop to get…supplies."

"Supplies?"

"You'll see."

Alex stopped at a shop called Escape to Eden on J Street, which piqued Dena's interest. The window of the store featured nothing more interesting than books and New Age CDs. What could staid Alex want in a counterculture haven like Escape to Eden?

Gently cupping her elbow as if she were made of porcelain, Alex helped her out of the Jag and onto her porch. Her house was silent. The twins were at preschool, and Irina would pick them up and deliver them home in several hours.

He brushed her hair with his lips. "I'm going to run a bath for you, and then I want you…in bed." He opened the door for her.

He wants me in bed. Her knees went so weak she almost fell over. "And…and then?"

His eyes filled with an overwhelming tenderness.

"And then I'll pamper you like you've never been pampered before."

Dena couldn't believe this was happening. At the beginning of her third trimester, she looked like a manatee. Did her half sister's husband want to make love to her? This couldn't be right. Had she fallen into an alternative universe? "Uh, Alex—"

He stopped her with a finger on her lips. "Don't worry." His voice dropped to a whisper. His finger rubbed back and forth across her mouth. She couldn't help trembling at his touch. "Everything is going to be perfect."

He helped her up the stairs and into her bedroom, then ran the bath while she sat on her bed. The mysterious package from Escape to Eden went into the bathroom with him.

"Get undressed." Alex emerged from the bathroom and handed her a towel, then disappeared again.

With difficulty, she pulled her sweatshirt over her head and unlaced her shoes. Leaning over stressed her back, so she tugged off her jeans, socks and underwear in one quick motion.

Through the open window, Dena could hear the click of Goldie's paws as the dog walked across the porch to her favorite mat. A slight breeze slipped through the casement, carrying the dry, spicy smell of autumn leaves.

A few minutes later, Alex said, "I'm ready for you now."

Wrapped in a bath towel, she looked up from her seat on her queen-size bed, covered with a pieced quilt she'd made herself. The job had filled the long, lonely nights while she'd been pregnant with the twins.

Alex had taken off his jacket and tie, loosened his

collar and cuffs. He'd undone several buttons of his starched shirt, revealing a soft fluff of golden hair. He looked adorably rumpled.

Hesitantly, she followed him into the bathroom. He'd switched off the bright overhead light; candles dimly illuminated the room, turning the functional space into a romantic, magical cave.

"Oh, Alex," she breathed.

The bath billowed with jasmine-scented bubbles. He kissed her hair again. "In you go."

He helped her clamber into the tub, then politely turned his head while she dropped the towel and slid into the aromatic water. She leaned against the back of the freestanding, claw-foot tub.

"Unusual to see this kind of bathtub." Alex urged her to lean her head back against the curved rim.

He'd placed a washcloth there to cushion her neck. "I loved it from the moment I saw it," she said. "I'd envisioned long, relaxing baths, but with the twins—" She shrugged. Beneath the bubbles, the water rippled from her movements.

"So you and Steve never did this?" His voice was low and intimate in her ear as he massaged her head.

"No. Did you and Tamara?"

"No. We didn't have a nice big tub like this one."

"Alex, this is wonderful. Thank you."

He laughed softly. "I've only just started." His fingers traveled up and down her neck, loosening the taut muscles. He reached for the Escape to Eden bag and withdrew a small plastic bottle of an orange-colored liquid.

"What's that?"

"A tangerine-scented massage oil."

Massage oil. Yum. "Er, why tangerine?"

"No reason. It just sounded nice."

And it *was* nice. Very, very nice. Much better than nice. She wondered how she'd rinse it out of her hair, then decided she didn't care, she'd just leave it. She closed her eyes and let Alex's clever fingers lull her into total relaxation. After he finished with her neck, he moved down each arm to her hands, massaging the pads of each finger separately.

She'd thought that Steve Randolph was a skilled lover. She'd wanted him because of how he made her feel. But she realized that he wasn't half as sensual as Alex. Alex touched her as though nothing else in the world existed, caressing every millimeter of flesh on her hands, relaxing each and every muscle fiber.

He gave her pleasure beyond sex. She'd never felt so cherished.

Dena noticed that the water had cooled. She said, "I think I'm ready to get out of the tub."

Alex reappeared. Having slipped into semiconscious bliss, she hadn't realized he'd left the room. "Let me help you. I don't want you to slip on the oil."

He held her arm and a towel as she struggled to her feet, her belly and her limp muscles making her clumsy. She guessed that neither the remains of the foam nor the towel completely hid her body, heavy with his child. What did Alex think of her? Did he find her attractive? She remembered that her looks didn't matter to Alex, that *she* mattered to Alex…because of the baby she carried.

Dena didn't know if she liked or hated that truth.

He guided her over to her bed. She saw that he'd turned her bedroom into a romantic bower, lit by scented pink candles, warm and cozy. "Lie down on your tummy, Dena, if you can."

"Not really. It's—it's not comfortable. It'll work with pillows, though."

"Let's try this." He stacked pillows under her head and breasts, then under her hips, creating a space to cradle her stomach.

"That's much better."

He draped another towel over her, covering her from waist to toes. "You get cold feet, right?"

"I'm surprised you remember." Her feet had become chilled on implant day.

"I remember everything about you, Dena." Was that love in his voice? She didn't dare hope that he returned her feelings.

His hands slid over her upper back. She smelled fresh tangerines. She closed her eyes, again letting herself slip into a fragrant, hazy dream world where nothing existed but Alex and his hands making her feel so good.

He worked down her back until he reached the spot she'd pulled. Despite the soreness, his touch sent sensual shivers through her. He lifted the towel to expose her legs, then massaged her thighs. She buried her face in the pillows and let relaxation ripple through her body.

"Good." Alex's whisper was soft and mesmerizing in her ear. His hands worked lower, kneading one calf and then the other. "Now, let's take care of these dogs. You really ought to spend more time with your feet up." He spent several minutes on each foot, paying special attention to the soles.

"I'm going to work on that sore back again. I'll be very gentle, I promise."

She believed him. She stayed relaxed when his hands moved to her lower back, gently probing the knotted muscles. He took his time massaging them into softness, then ran his fingers up to her hair.

He played with it until desire ignited within her again. *Control yourself, Dena,* she told herself sternly. *This massage is for the mother of his child, not for you.* She took several deep, calming breaths.

"Good. Now, go to sleep."

She stirred reluctantly. "The twins—"

"I'll call Irina and together we'll take care of the kids. Don't worry."

As he left, Dena snuggled her face into the pillows and tried to remember all the reasons why she shouldn't fall in love with Alex Chandler.

Softly closing the door to Dena's bedroom, Alex walked quietly down the hall. He went downstairs to the kitchen in search of a beer. At the refrigerator, he stopped, arrested by the sight of new fridge art drawn by the twins.

Not surprisingly, Miriam's drawing held a big-eared mouse. Jack's picture featured a big house with four stick figures—one labeled Alex—and something brown with four legs, sort of like a dog.

Alex smiled. The mad tea party, which he'd attended as Big Bird, hadn't been a fluke. As far as the kids were concerned, he was part of this family.

After swigging a healthy gulp of his beer, he picked up the phone to update Irina, who agreed to keep the twins overnight. He then called Greg. As luck would have it, Greg's youngest brother, a student at Sac State, needed a part-time job and could work for Dena.

Pleased with the afternoon's accomplishments, Alex took his beer out to the veranda. Goldie, curled on her mat, thumped her tail in greeting but didn't get up.

In the autumn dusk, Dena's yard remained as lovely a place as in the summer. The oaks, timelessly grand, framed the garden, while late roses continued to bloom. Smaller deciduous trees and shrubs had started to turn vivid shades of yellow and red, splashes of color against the dark backdrop.

Everything in his life was falling into place, like a well-structured tax shelter. He remembered something Irina had said weeks before, at Greg's wedding: "I have a feeling my Tamara planned everything that's happened."

Had his sweet, manipulative wife set him up with her half sister? Alex recalled that one of Tamara's greatest worries during her final illness was his fate after her death. At the time, he hadn't wanted to discuss the issue, refusing to accept what she knew as fact: that she was going to die and leave him alone.

He sipped his beer. He still missed Tami, but recognized that the surrogacy had dragged him from the depths of his despair. He'd been forced to care about the welfare of others—Dena, the twins and his baby—rather than wallow in grief.

He raised his bottle to salute his late wife. "To you, Tami. You were one smart lady."

His thoughts turned to Dena. Everything about her— the smoothness of her satiny skin, her female scent, the lushness of her voluptuous body, big and beautiful with his child—reminded him he'd grown back his libido. Reining in his desire during the massage had been one tough job.

Alex took out his pad of paper and flipped to the pro-and-con list he'd started. On the "pro" side, he wrote: "a total sex goddess."

But what difference could that make? He glanced at his list. The items on the "con" side still had to stop him in his tracks. He'd be insane to have a romance with the surrogate mother of his child.

So much was at stake. It was as though Dena held the brass ring as he spun around a carousel. Home, children and family were the treasures he sought.

If the relationship failed… He winced. His heart was in danger, yes, but that was the least of his concerns. What of the twins? Already attached to him, they'd be hurt if he and Dena became estranged. Unacceptable.

For the good of the baby, he'd already made plans that could prove troublesome in the future. Living with Dena and the twins after the child's birth. Frequent future visits. He bet—no, he *knew*—that Dena would tell him every second how to raise his child.

He firmed his resolve. He'd keep close tabs on Dena, but he was absolutely *not* going to fall in love with her.

Chapter Eleven

"You did *what?*" The next morning, Dena spread a piece of wheat toast with ricotta cheese, then topped it with salsa.

Alex looked at her breakfast with a wince. "Look, Randy Holloway is a nice kid, and he'll work hard for you."

"That's not the issue."

Dena's pleasure over the massage had turned to irritation when she discovered that he'd offered Greg's brother a job in her business. "Alex, I know you meant well, but you shouldn't have butted in."

"It's just for a few months, until the baby's born and you're back on your feet." He reached into her pantry for corn flakes.

She sat at her table with a sigh. "You really don't get it, do you? What if I hired someone to work in your business?"

"I'm not pregnant with an IVF baby. Besides, what

were you going to do?'' He poured cereal into a bowl, then topped it with milk.

She pressed her lips together. ''Find some college kid to do the physical labor. I remember what the doctor said.''

Alex brought his bowl over to the table and took a chair opposite her. ''So it's done. I thought you said that there would be no more arguments.''

She tried to frown at him but couldn't. Worse, she couldn't stop her lips from twitching with repressed laughter. ''You are really quite a piece of work, you know that?''

He grinned. ''Tamara told me that all the time.''

The remark dashed her mood as though he'd dumped ice water down her blouse, reminding her that he was her sister's husband. When she'd awakened to discover Alex asleep in the guest room, she found herself encouraged by this new level of intimacy. Their relationship had grown in leaps and bounds during the last twenty-four hours, so much so that she'd allowed herself to dream of a life with Alex always by her side.

But now she'd been reminded that Alex was Tami's, not hers.

Oblivious to the chaos in her heart, Alex crunched corn flakes in his mouth, chewed and swallowed. ''I phoned the medical center to find out about Lamaze classes.''

''Oh.'' Oh, no. Lamaze classes could be unbearably intimate. You sat on a mat with your partner, looked into each other's eyes, breathed together. She really didn't want Alex to be her Lamaze coach. ''Are you sure you want to do that? It's—it's quite a time commitment. Mom already knows how to do it.''

He looked at her with an odd expression in his eyes. "Are you trying to get rid of me? Of course I'm sure."

A week later, Dena entered the Lamaze class together with Alex. The first time she'd taken this course, she'd been undercut by a sense of inferiority, with her mother instead of her husband accompanying her. Now, with Alex by her side, she felt like a phony. It wasn't her fault, but she knew everyone would think they were married and enjoying a normal pregnancy.

The room filled quickly with several other couples. The instructor, a petite young Asian named Wanda, closed the blinds, shutting out the gray afternoon.

Clad in jeans, Alex sat cross-legged on a mat next to her. With a jolt, Dena realized that she'd never before seen Alex in jeans. He looked great, the faded denim hugging his muscular, taut thighs. He wrapped an arm around her as the instructor gave the familiar talk about breathing.

"Face your partner," Wanda said.

Alex moved quickly so Dena wouldn't have to shift. She appreciated that. "Thank you," she whispered.

"Anything for you, honey." He gave her a smile.

Her heart soared. *Anything for you, honey.*

On Wanda's direction, Dena and the other women drew in short, quick breaths.

"Remember, we're breathing for our baby." Wanda walked around the room, stopping near Alex and Dena. She eyed Alex. "Move closer to your partner."

Alex scooted closer, until the side of his body touched Dena's.

She leaned toward him and closed her eyes. She breathed in the now-familiar aroma of his lime-scented aftershave. Her body heated with the warm, sensual bliss she always felt when she neared Alex. She wanted him so much she thought she'd faint.

She couldn't ignore the impact that Alex had on her body and heart any longer. They had to talk about it. "Alex—" she began, opening her eyes.

Wanda interrupted. "Keep eye contact with your partner. Hold hands. Breathe."

Alex took Dena's hands in his. She wasn't a small woman, but his hands overwhelmed hers. She rubbed her thumbs over the fine, blond hairs on the backs, reveling in their slight scratchiness. Another thrill leaped through her, electric and powerful as lightning.

She looked into his eyes. He stared back at her, his gaze honest and candid. She read trust in Alex's blue orbs.

She couldn't tell him. He relied upon her to fulfill her agreement to carry his and Tamara's baby to term. Falling in love wasn't part of the deal and would complicate the situation too much.

The baby kicked. Dena pulled his hand toward her abdomen, clad in a purple tunic over black leggings. "He's saying 'hi' to his dad."

Alex made wide circles on her tummy with his palm. "Hi to you, too, baby."

"*Effleurage*, very good." Wanda raised her voice. "Partners, you may massage Mommy's stomach with a circular motion. This is called *effleurage* and is very relaxing."

"Relaxing, my foot," Dena muttered. Desire tensed her muscles and flickered along her skin.

"What did you say?" he asked.

"Nothing."

"Breathe, Dena. Breathe for our baby."

Our baby. Did he realize what he'd said? Probably not.

"Give me some pant breathing now." Wanda circled the floor like a dog shepherding lambs, watching her charges.

Dena obediently panted while Alex held her hands. They looked into each other's eyes. *Big mistake.* She couldn't concentrate while staring into Alex's blue gaze, boundlessly warm as the sky in June. She wanted to kiss him until he trembled the same way he made her quiver and shake.

Wanda's tone shifted. "Visualize your cervix opening."

Alex's hands jerked in Dena's grasp. "I'll pass," he muttered.

She stifled her laughter. "Wanda means me," she murmured demurely.

"All right, I'll visualize *your* cervix opening."

"Umm." Closing her eyes, Dena tried to visualize. But what did a cervix look like? Her mind wandered to a fantasy of Alex caressing her breasts into stiff, sensitive peaks while she— *Cut this out, Dena!*

She opened her eyes to see Alex watching her, a slight smile on his face. "How's it going? That cervix open yet?"

"Uh, yeah." Dena felt her face reddening. She'd better get back to the approved set of visions.

"Let's do some timing exercises now. Dads, do all of you have a watch with a second hand?" Wanda asked.

Alex pushed back the sleeve of his green sweater to reveal his watch, a high-tech digital timepiece. "Hmm. I guess I can count the seconds."

Wanda distributed pencils and paper to all who needed them. "Let's pretend that Mom is feeling an early contraction. Moms, start to breathe. Dads, write down the time.''

Dena panted until she started to feel light-headed. She stopped.

''Breathe, honey. You're not breathing.''

''Alex, I'm about to pass out.''

''Oh, my God. Put your head between your knees.''

''It's not that bad. I just don't want to hyperventilate.''

''Now we're later in the labor and the contractions are coming faster.'' Wanda's strident tones interrupted their conversation. ''Another one starting…now!''

Alex wrote down the time while Dena huffed.

''The contractions are now five minutes apart and they're very intense. Dads, what do you do?''

''Take her to the hospital!'' the men chorused.

''Right!'' Wanda beamed. ''And don't forget the overnight bag!''

After the Lamaze class, they picked up the twins and took them to the park. Restless after they'd been confined in the car, the twins tumbled out of the Jag moments after Alex parked. Screeching, they made beelines for a jungle gym. Alex held Dena's arm, following at a more sedate pace.

Little recommended the chill, gray day except that it wasn't raining. Even the short, sparse grass between the parking lot and the playground seemed leached of color. The twins' bright, plush jackets—red for Miri, blue for Jack—lent life to the drab afternoon.

Dena sat heavily on one of the gray concrete benches near the sandy play area. Alex stood behind her and rubbed her shoulder. Behind him, he heard the sound of a car approach, then stop in the parking lot. Another child dashed past them, a little boy slightly bigger than Jack, heading toward the swings.

Alex felt Dena's muscles bunch beneath his fingers. "What's wrong?"

"Maybe nothing," she responded, her gaze still on her kids.

Shoes crunched on gravel. Alex turned his head to see a blond woman approach, dressed in tight capris and a sweater.

"Hi, Dena." The blonde ran her tongue over her lower lip, glossy with makeup. "Who's your friend?"

Dena stood. Her icy stare passed over the blonde as though the space remained empty. "Alex, I'm going to take a walk down by the river. Watch Jack and Miri, will you?" Dena walked away without waiting for an answer.

Alex gawked at her departing back. He knew her to be the friendliest of souls. What on earth—

The blonde called, "You should drop your hostility, Dena! All that negative baggage hurts no one but yourself!" The woman sighed and said to Alex, "She really needs to get over the past. We used to be such good friends. By the way, I'm Sarah Vanellis. I also live on Shadownook." She stuck out a hand.

"Alex Chandler." Taking her hand, he shook it, repressing a wince as she dug in her long fingernails.

Her brown eyes widened. "Oh, you're Tamara's ex, huh?" She didn't let go.

Alex stiffened, tugging his hand away. "Tamara isn't my ex-wife, she was my wife."

The woman shrugged. "Ex-wife, wife, what's the difference?" She chuckled, giving Alex a sidelong glance through long, dark lashes.

As far as Alex was concerned, her attempt at humor

fell flat. "Excuse me." He strode over to the jungle gym, pretending to supervise the kids.

No wonder Dena left. Alex had never encountered someone so tactless. Occasionally, a day passed that he didn't recall his wife with a pang, but he still missed Tamara. This Vanellis woman had ripped the healing wound in his heart wide open.

Dena hadn't returned, so Alex endured several uncomfortable minutes until Sarah Vanellis left with her son. Then Miri—a welcome distraction—tired of the jungle gym and demanded that Unka Alex push her on the swings.

Jack hung upside down from the topmost bar of the jungle gym. *He'll be a great gymnast one day,* Alex thought. He envisioned adult Jack, pecs sweaty, competing in and winning the Olympics. Alex grinned at his own wild fantasies. One dividend of the surrogacy was that he'd grown much closer to the twins. He couldn't imagine loving any children more.

He left Miri for a moment to open his pad to the Dena pro-con list. Beneath "pro," he wrote "good parent." No questions there. The twins were occasionally unruly, but perhaps that was the nature of some kids. Hopefully his baby would be a calmer child. He'd make sure of it.

He noticed that the "pro" side had become a much longer list than "con."

Dena reappeared in the distance and he hastily put away the pad. He had the feeling that spontaneous Dena wouldn't understand his methodical issue analysis.

He couldn't tear his glance away from her as she approached. Clad in form-fitting black leggings, her legs remained shapely despite her pregnancy. Her long purple shirt clung to every curve, lovingly outlining her large, high breasts. He could see the sweet outline of her belly pressed against the fabric, rounded with his child.

Alex sucked in a breath, his mouth dry. *Steady, Chandler,* he cautioned himself. *We're close, so very close. Stay the course!*

He swallowed. "Thanks for leaving me to deal with that woman."

"There are some people I just don't care to talk with."

"I'll grant that Sarah Vanellis is obnoxious, but I've never seen you deliberately shun someone before. That's not like you."

He was met with silence.

"What did she do that was so bad?" he asked.

A bitter laugh broke from Dena's throat. "Oh, nothing much. Nothing that a lot of other women in my neighborhood didn't do."

Alex's jaw tightened. He could guess what Sarah Vanellis and the other women Dena knew had done—with Dena's husband. "I'm sorry."

She shrugged. "First he went up one side of Shadownook and did all the women there. Bink—bink—bink—bink." Her index finger made little lines in the air. "Then he went down the other side. Bink—bink—bink."

"Don't you mean boink—boink—boink?"

She looked surprised before she broke out in laughter. "Yeah, I guess you're right." She controlled her guffaws. "He went up and down the street, boinking all the way."

He glanced down at her. She was damp-eyed from either tears or laughter, but he couldn't tell which.

She continued, "I'm surprised I can laugh about it. He used to make me so angry—" She drew in a short, tense breath. "I never thought I'd lose that rage, it was so consuming."

"You sure you're over him?"

"I don't want him back, if that's what you mean." Her answer came swift as a shot and as reassuring as hot chocolate on a frosty night. "But as far as forgiveness goes, no way. Not Steve or any of my so-called *friends.*" She spat out the word as if it tasted bad.

"I don't understand someone like Steve. How dishonest and disrespectful. And why get married if you're going to fool around?" He sat down on the bench and tugged on Dena's hand until she joined him.

She gave his hand a little squeeze before she answered. "He didn't fool around. Not at first. He swore I was the only woman he'd ever love. But my pregnancy changed everything."

"Had the two of you discussed children?"

"Of course. But Steve was more talk than action in the emotional arena, I think. He was pretty immature. So was I. Having a child was this—this big experiment. Maybe he could have dealt with only one baby, but he went into shock when we discovered I carried twins. That was when he started the boinkfest. So I confronted him."

"What did he say?" Alex eyed the twins. He was pretty sure they didn't need to hear this conversation. But they still seemed absorbed in play, slithering up and down the slide.

"Denied everything, but I trust the woman who snitched on him. He couldn't explain how she knew about a birthmark on a very intimate part of his anatomy."

Alex winced in sympathy with Dena. He put an arm around her shoulders.

"Then he left." She snuggled against his side, a cuddly, warm armful.

He couldn't resist hugging her closer. Her presence in his life brightened every gray day, lighting a fire in him he couldn't resist. But he also wanted to discover all Dena's hidden hurts, expose them so they'd lose their virulence. "How did you get along after he went?"

She smiled wistfully. "I'm not sure, but I somehow muddled through. I was eighteen when Steve and I met. I thought I'd be with him forever. But now, ten years later, I realize that I wanted him for all the wrong reasons—because he was fun, and exciting, and made every day into a new adventure. Life with Steve didn't have much to do with the reality of raising kids. But it's hard for me to have regrets."

The shouts of the twins broke into their conversation. "Mommy! Look at us now!" Miriam flung herself down the slide headfirst, followed by Jack. The children ended up at the bottom of the slide in a happy jumble of children, jackets and mittens.

"See what I mean?" Dena's eyes misted. "If it weren't for Steve, there'd be no Jack and Miri. Unthinkable."

He caressed her hand. "It couldn't have been easy, two kids and only one parent."

"It wasn't. On the other hand, no one argued with my decisions."

Alex let her go and moved a couple of inches away. She'd had a free hand with the twins, which meant that she'd definitely be bossy about his child. He made a mental note to add this factor to the "con" side of the list. "Didn't Irina help?"

"Sure, Mom helped me out a lot, but she believed that it was important for me to make mistakes and learn from them.'' She grinned. ''The Irina Cohen theory of parenting.''

He smiled back. ''Sounds pretty good. I'm getting excited about my own adventure into fatherhood.''

''Alex, it's the greatest. I'm truly happy for you.'' She pressed his hand where it lay on the cool concrete bench. ''I know you'll be a great daddy.''

We'll be great, he wanted to say, but he hesitated. Maybe Dena was over Steve. But had he grown beyond the pain of losing Tamara?

Chapter Twelve

Later, after the kids were in bed, Alex helped Dena prepare mint tea. He carried their mugs to the coffee table in the living room before building a fire in the hearth against the cool October evening.

Dena curled up on the leather couch, cradling her mug. "Mom's going to be out of town for Halloween. Could you help me out with the kids?"

"Of course. Gallivanting around the neighborhood at night isn't healthy for someone in your condition. Shouldn't you be in bed, resting?" Alex sipped his tea and eyed the crackling fire, hoping the big log he'd put on it would catch.

She huffed. "You just want to get me into the sack," she joked, setting down her tea on the burled coffee table nearby.

Months of the flirting and the on-again, off-again intimacy had stretched Alex's patience to the breaking point. Regardless of the risks, he decided to take a stand.

He thumped down his mug onto the table with a clatter. Striding to her, he planted one arm on each side of her face, caging her against the back of the couch.

Bringing his lips to within a fraction of an inch from hers, he said, "Count on it."

Dena gasped. Alex's eyes, gleaming with a blue fire, seized her gaze and didn't let go. The intense scrutiny reached inside of her to grip her soul.

She couldn't move. She couldn't speak. She didn't know how to respond.

His breath, pleasantly scented by the mint tea, wafted into her nostrils. The package of tea had advertised the mint as "stimulating." That was no lie; a sensual tremor, hotter than August, flickered through her body.

If she leaned forward, just a bit, her mouth would touch his. Did she dare?

Maybe not, but he did. He stroked his lips over hers, back and forth, in the lightest of caresses. "Remember Greg's wedding?"

She nodded. Need coursed through her, still binding her voice.

"When we kissed?"

She forced out a whisper. "I—I can't stop thinking about it."

"Well, think about this." Alex nibbled her lower lip, seeking entrance.

Her heartbeat went crazy. She didn't know if this was right, but she couldn't deny him. Liquid fire blazed deep in her body. She closed her eyes and kissed him back, enjoying the thrust and parry of their tongues. The creak of leather followed by his warm weight by her side told her that he'd sat next to her on the couch. Then he gathered her—all of her, even her big belly—into his arms. His free hand played with the hair near her temple.

She shivered with want, his tenderness exciting her

more than Steve's touch ever had. Alex's hand slid lower, toying with the opening of her chenille robe before he cupped her breast through her thin nightgown, testing its tender weight in his palm. Her nerves sang with desire.

"You're trembling." Alex's thumb danced over her nipple, rimming it. She felt her breast quiver. When he closed his hand softly over the sensitive flesh, she thought she'd come apart.

He lay her back against the side cushions of the couch and covered her in a full-body embrace that ignited her from head to heels. Reveling in the lean, hard form pinning her to the couch, she ran her hands across his chest and down his sides, learning his body, savoring each plane and curve of muscle.

He feathered his lips along her face until he reached the tiny pulse that beat in the hollow of her throat. While veiling the sensitive skin with kisses, he continued to caress her breast. Easing his weight off hers, he parted her robe, exposing her body to his gaze.

With a frantic squeak, she tried to pull the halves of the robe together. Her panties and short nightgown, stretched over her belly, didn't hide much.

He stopped her. "No, Dena. Please." He unfastened one snap, then two, then opened the gown to examine her breasts with ravenous eyes. He bent his head to kiss her nipple, running the ridge of his teeth over the aroused tip.

She moaned aloud. "You can't want to look at me like…like this."

"Like what? Pregnant with my child?" He stroked her belly, then explored lower, to her sensitive inner thighs. He caressed her gently. She couldn't repress the wild cry that rose from her throat.

He'd already loosened his collar and tie, so now she reached for his starched white shirt, yanking the buttons free from their holes. She slipped her hand inside his shirt to find heaven, the broad, strong chest she'd dreamed of since she'd seen his naked torso so many months ago, displayed on her bed like a Greek god come to call.

She rubbed her palm across the golden curls dusting his pecs, taking sensual delight in their masculine coarseness. Dena had forgotten how wonderful loving could be. Alex made everything new, erasing Steve from her consciousness as though he'd never been her lover. She pulled Alex closer, sliding her tongue in his mouth, begging for another of his deep, sweet soul kisses.

Pressing intimately against him, she gasped with wanton longing and was about to succumb to his seduction when he said, "You're carrying my baby, Dena. That makes you beautiful to me."

She wrenched herself away. "No! Not like that!" In tears, she struggled to her feet.

He sat back on the couch. The passion glazing his eyes faded, a puzzled expression replacing it. "What? What did I say? We've been getting along so well—"

"I don't want to be wanted because I'm your brood mare, Alex." The shock and hurt slashed her to the core.

"That's—that's not how it is at all." Alex sounded as stunned as she. "You're beautiful. You've always been beautiful. I just never saw it before."

She scrubbed her hands over her face. "You didn't see me because of Tamara. You're my sister's husband. Perhaps this just isn't meant to be."

"People told me that about our baby, too. I didn't believe that, and I don't accept this!" Rising, he adjusted his sweater.

He curved a hand around her head, again playing with her hair.

She jerked away.

His hand dropped. "I guess I've given you a lot to think about."

"That you have," she managed to say.

"I'll leave now. I'll see you again on Halloween, at dusk."

He gave her a quick, hard kiss before he left, again jolting her all the way through.

She didn't move. She couldn't twitch a muscle until she heard the throaty purr of the Jag as Alex drove away. Then she sank down on the couch, trembling.

His kisses had been better than before, richer because of their spontaneity. The wedding kiss had been planned; this was impulsive.

But he hadn't wanted to kiss her, Dena Cohen Randolph, mother of two and semiemployed gardener. In some peculiar act of masculine possession, he'd wanted to have the mother of his child.

The knowledge that any surrogate would have been okay for Alex made her want to scream. She bit her lower lip as she let the tears flow.

She'd see him again in just a few days. How could she face him? She felt belittled, humiliated.

After groping for a tissue in the pocket of her robe, she blew her nose, telling herself she shouldn't feel ashamed. She hadn't done anything wrong.

"He's clueless," she muttered to herself as she dumped the cold tea in the sink. "Forget about him!"

Dressed as a clown, Jack carried an orange plastic pumpkin with a black strap. Miriam wore a Minnie

Mouse outfit complete with round black ears and a funny, patent-leather bag for her treats.

Dena, attired as a ghost, had draped a white sheet over her swollen body, covering herself completely. There'd be no illicit peeking tonight. Her defenses were up. She tapped an impatient toe on the front porch as everyone waited for Alex at dusk on Halloween night.

He tore into the drive, gravel spitting from beneath the Jag's tires. After he exited his car, she saw that he wore a three-piece suit.

"What are you dressed as, an accountant?" she asked as he drew near.

A grin split his face. "Yes, I've been pretending to do this job for quite a while." He glanced down. "And who are these people?" he asked Dena. "I didn't know you were going to invite a clown and a mousie over tonight, Dena."

The twins giggled. "It's *us,* Unka Alex." Miriam waved her gloved hand, narrowly missing her brother's red, shiny clown-nose.

Jack ducked. "Let's go. I heard from Nicky Vanellis that his mom has candy apples."

Dena tensed. She glanced at Alex. "We usually go around the other block."

"Can we go on Shadownook tonight, Mommy?" Miriam pressed up against Dena's side. "Plee-eeze?"

Dena sighed. "Alex, could you please take the kids up and down Shadownook? I'll stay here and give out candy to the trick-or-treaters who come by."

Alex nodded, hoping he looked sympathetic and understanding.

"Just make sure that all the candy they get is wrapped." Dena waved at them as they left.

While he walked with the twins from house to house,

inspecting the treats they collected, he considered the situation with Dena. Alex blamed himself and his clumsiness; he'd mishandled her badly. But it wasn't entirely his fault. He hadn't wooed a woman since he'd met Tamara in college, many long years ago, and their relationship had been smooth sailing. Neither had ever harbored a single doubt about their love.

But Dena was an entirely different story. He didn't know what she needed.

Jack had capered ahead, while Miriam stood uncertainly at the end of an unlit, slate walkway. Luminous, green "spiderwebs" laced the porch at the end of the path. Fake skulls glowed. Alex removed a small flashlight, attached to his key ring, from his pocket and clicked on its button to illuminate the way for his niece.

Reassured, Miriam skipped along the slate to the porch and got her candy apple, which fell with a *plunk* into her bag. The kids thanked Sarah Vanellis, who stood in the doorway of her home, waving.

The answer came to Alex as though a light had clicked on in his head. Reassurance.

That had to be what Dena needed. Though she denied it, Steve had ripped a hole in Dena's heart and ego the size of the Grand Canyon. As far as Alex knew, she hadn't dated since. He was the first man in whom she'd shown an interest in five years.

Dena cared about him. He was sure of that. While they'd kissed, her emerald eyes had shimmered with passion. When he'd cradled her lovely breast in his hand, her breath had come in short, sharp, aroused pants. The power of her response had left him stunned, craving completion only with her.

She'd been about to give herself to him until he'd

opened his stupid mouth and said exactly the wrong thing.

Though proud he'd figured her out, he cautioned himself. He couldn't just run to her and ask her forgiveness for being such a fool. He wouldn't win Dena, a determined, independent woman, unless he convinced her that he wanted her for herself and not because of the baby.

He rubbed his temple. Because his feelings had developed along with the fetus, persuading Dena that he truly wanted her wouldn't be easy. Plus, he'd lied to himself and to Dena for so long. Denying his feelings for her, he'd said over and over that he was caring for the baby's welfare when actually she was the one who'd drawn his concern. He'd made his task doubly hard.

But he'd do it. He had to. His happiness and that of his family was at stake.

And the four of them—soon to be five—were his family.

"Hey, Unka Alex! Wanna bite?" Miriam held up her red candy apple. Reddish smears of the cinnamon-flavored sweet already adorned her face.

He swallowed. "That's all right, honey. You enjoy it."

After they finished the trick-or-treating on Shadownook, they returned home. The twins dumped their loot on the kitchen table.

"You got a pretty good haul," Dena said. "Mini Hershey bars, candy apples, sticks of gum—yum." She swept the lot into a large wooden bowl.

The kids howled. "That's ours!" Jack grabbed vainly for the bowl, which Dena held high, out of his reach.

"No way," she said firmly. "Remember what we talked about?"

"The tooth fairy will get mad if she comes and finds

holes in our teeth,'' Miriam piped up. ''So we get one piece a day.''

''Yeah, and you've already started your candy apples, so that's your one piece today.'' Dena set the bowl on top of the refrigerator. Alex noticed that Jack's picture of the four of them still hung on the fridge. Dena continued, ''Every day after preschool you may each have a candy.''

Jack pushed out his lower lip.

''Don't start with me, Jackie, or there'll be no candy at all.''

Jack produced a sunny grin.

''Good boy.'' She ruffled his hair and smiled at Alex. ''Now, finish your apples and go up to bed. Come on, Miri.''

Alex hoped that smile meant she didn't harbor a grudge. After reading to Jack and putting out his light, he returned to the living room to find Dena in her usual spot on the couch, curled up in her pink robe with a mug of hot apple cider.

He didn't say anything, but kindled a fire in the hearth.

Dena watched him, taut and tense. His broad shoulders, set off by his crisp white shirt and navy vest, irresistibly drew her gaze. He'd taken off his jacket, loosened his tie and rolled up his cuffs. The blond hairs on his muscular forearms glittered in the ruddy firelight.

She wondered if Alex would again make a play for her, and what she'd do.

Tomorrow would be the first day of November. Their baby was due on or about January the first, welcoming the New Year. Then Alex and the baby would move into her house. Alex would sleep just two doors away from her, in the baby's room.

A little while after the baby's birth—just six weeks, she'd read—she'd be ready again, at least physically. Ready to have sex. Ready to make love.

And Alex would be there.

She breathed deeply, aware of the desire pulsating through her body with every molecule of air, with every glance at Alex, kneeling by the hearth.

But how long would he stay? The question plagued her.

Intellectually, she believed he'd always be a part of her life. But her heart still harbored fear. After what he'd said the other night, she didn't know if she could trust him or herself.

Alex finished fiddling with the fire and came to her side, taking his place next to her on the couch. He wrapped an arm around her shoulders, bringing her close.

Dena knew she should pull away, but couldn't. The warmth of his embrace felt too good. With a little sigh, she let herself melt into his body, cuddling.

"I know I said the wrong thing the other night." His breath tickled her earlobe. "Can you just…forget it?"

She stirred. "That's something a woman can't easily forget."

"You'll have plenty of time to forget my stupidity," he said wryly. "There'll be other dumb things for you to overlook."

She gave a shaky little laugh. "Not like that, I hope."

"No, not like that. Dena, look at me, please."

She craned her head. She saw the caring in his eyes for a moment before he kissed her again, drawing her into a sensual dance that could have only one ending.

Dena's green eyes fluttered shut as she responded to his kiss with even more passion than she'd shown before. Her fragrance, flowery with a hint of womanly musk, filled his nostrils. His blood leaped through his veins.

Shuddering, she broke off the kiss, too soon, he felt. "We shouldn't be doing this. The children—"

"Aren't here. We are." He misted her neck with kisses, watching as lust clouded her eyes.

Dena sucked in a deep breath and somehow pulled away. She put a trembling hand to her lips, finding them swollen, sensitive. She ran the tip of her finger along the seam of her mouth.

He groaned. "Dena, please. For a woman who's saying no, you're pretty confusing."

"I am? I don't mean to be, really." She dropped her hand.

"Really." Disengaging himself, he strode to the door, all tall and golden and precious and oh, so Alex. He took her breath away.

"I have to be sure, Alex."

Hand on the doorknob, he turned, his hungry eyes roaming her body. She felt naked, defenseless. Her body throbbed with an unfulfilled need.

If he said a single word, she'd be his.

"I'll wait for you." The door slammed shut as he left.

Chapter Thirteen

On Thanksgiving Day Dena got up at 6:00 a.m., intending to space out her tasks over the hours until her guests were scheduled to arrive, but found herself dawdling.

Thank heavens for her mother. She'd volunteered to pick up the twins from preschool on Wednesday afternoon and keep them most of the day. Responsible for the turkey, Irina would bring the twins over at three o'clock, when the festivities would begin. Alex said he'd arrive at two, to help set the table and cook some of the side dishes, but Dena didn't want to shove all the work onto him.

After putting on a baggy dress that made her look like a pink hippo, Dena's first stop was the baby's room.

Alex had bought a new mattress for the crib and a comfy, padded rocker for her to use while nursing. Neither had wanted to learn the gender of the baby before birth, so he'd purchased sheets suitable for a boy or a girl. He'd picked a lively Donald Duck print.

She sat in the rocker. These days, everything seemed to make her tired. Though due the first week in January, her baby had dropped early, alarming Dr. Mujedin. He'd put her on a regimen of partial bed rest and medications to delay birth and to accelerate development of the baby's lungs, in case a premature labor couldn't be avoided. The drugs made her weary and ill most of the time.

Alex had been wonderfully supportive, by her side every spare minute. Their good-night kisses had grown longer and more passionate. Her physical condition— and two nosy, impressionable four-year-olds—had stymied any greater intimacy. She loved him more and more each day, but didn't trust her feelings, or his. So she bit back the words of love whenever they slipped to the tip of her tongue.

The baby moved, and Dena caressed her stomach. Lately, her child seemed to relish exercise in the mornings. However, today she sensed a different quality to the kicks and pushes. Months ago, he swam freely around her womb. Now the baby squirmed as though cramped.

"You can hardly wait to get born, huh, kiddo?" she whispered to her baby. "Well, Mommy wants you out, too. I'm eager to meet you, darling."

With a jolt, Dena realized what she'd been saying.

This was her baby. Though this child carried her sister's genes, it was Dena's blood and marrow that had nourished him since April, eight long months ago. She'd be the one to give birth and life to him; her breasts would feed him.

This was her baby. She'd never give up this child.

She thrust a closed fist to her mouth in horror. *Alex.* Oh, God, this was Alex's baby, the child that he and

Tamara had sweated blood to have. He needed a family more than she. How could she think of depriving him of this joy?

"He'll hate me if I break my word," she whispered aloud.

She remembered what he'd said when they discussed Steve. "How dishonest." Alex had always been scrupulously truthful with Dena and with everyone, especially about the baby. He'd made his position clear. He and the baby would stay for a while after the birth and then...

Dena curled into a tight, unhappy ball as hot tears flooded her eyes. She didn't know how she could let either of them go when the time came.

Sharp pain rippled across her abdomen as wetness washed her thighs. She screamed aloud. "Oh, my God! My water's breaking!"

She staggered through the house searching for a portable phone. Where had Jack and Miri hidden them this time? She waddled as fast as she could into her room, where she located one on her dresser. She punched in Alex's number with frantic fingers.

"Alex, get over here right away."

"Huh?"

Darn him, he was still asleep. "Hurry up!" she shrieked. "Do you want me to call 911?"

His voice sharpened. "Is it time?"

"Yes!"

"Are you all right?"

"Yes, I'm all right! I'm going to have a baby!" She slammed the phone down. She yanked off the wet garments she wore and used them to dry herself, then put on another hippo dress. Grabbing shoes, she stumbled downstairs, then noticed that the contraction had ended minutes ago.

She stopped in her tracks, taking deep, calming breaths. Goldie scratched at the door, so Dena let her in. Her dog snuffled at her hand, searching for food.

"Oh, yeah," Dena muttered. She fed the dog, then washed her hands and retrieved the packed overnight bag from the hall closet.

A screech of tires heralded Alex's arrival. He pounded her front door open while still talking on his cell phone. "Yes, I'm at her house. I'll see you at Sutter Hospital in a few minutes." He clicked off the phone.

"Who was that?" she asked.

"Dr. Mujedin. Get in the car. How frequent are the contractions?" He took the bag from her hand and slammed the door behind her.

"I don't know, but my water broke so I bet it's time. I don't want to take any chances."

He bundled her into the Jag. "Dammit, Dena, it's barely thirty-four weeks." His voice cracked with tension.

"I know." Full-term was thirty-seven or thirty-eight weeks. Their baby was too young to come into the world.

"Anemia, jaundice, underdeveloped lungs, sleep apnea—"

"Alex, please!"

"I'm sorry, but I'm scared. I wanted our baby to be perfect." He made the left onto Fair Oaks too fast.

Our baby. The phrase should have sounded lovely, but it tore through Dena's heart like jagged glass. She took a deep breath. "Listen, no child is perfect. Not even… yours."

His fingers clenched the steering wheel, the knuckles

white. He must have pressed harder on the accelerator, because the car seemed to leap forward, like the animal for which it had been named.

Alex stopped the car at the ER door with a squeal of brakes. An orderly, who'd been waiting for them, helped Dena into a wheelchair and whisked her away.

While he parked, Alex pulled out his cell phone and made a few quick phone calls. "You and the twins will have to celebrate Thanksgiving by yourselves, Irina. I don't know how long Dena's labor will last."

Irina sounded amazingly calm. "Don't worry, Alex, dahlink. Everything will be fine. She's a healthy girl."

"The baby's too early. Thirty-four weeks." He wiped his sweaty face with a handkerchief.

"Eight months, Alex, and Sutter is a great hospital with wonderful doctors. The baby will be all right, you'll see. Perhaps we'll come down and wait with you."

"Oh, you don't have to do that."

"Of course I do. This is my grandchild we're talking about. What can I bring you?"

"Uh, I haven't eaten yet. Let's eat breakfast when you get here."

"*Ciao,* dahlink." She hung up the phone, leaving Alex shaking his head in disbelief. He'd never heard of a Jewish grandmother who said *ciao* as though she'd just stcppcd off a plane from Rome.

He chuckled, realizing anew that he truly loved his wife's family. "Thank you, Tami," he said softly as he dialed his parents.

Patricia told him that Leighton was playing an early morning golf game. "We'll drive out as soon as he gets home."

Alex could hear stress in his mother's high, quavery

voice. Perhaps she had decided in her heart to love her grandchild. "Don't worry, Mom."

"I just don't want you to get hurt, son."

"Everything will be all right." Alex struggled to keep his composure. "I'll see you soon."

Finally at the OB ward, he discovered Dena settled in a birthing room. "What's going on?"

"I'm already dilated to six centimeters. This baby's gonna come fast." She leaned back into the pillows.

He sat down by her side and took her hand, avoiding her IV. "Like Jack and Miri."

"I'm serious. If you want to be there, think about scrubbing up."

"What's with this room?" He looked around. In contrast to the tumult outside, Dena's room was dimly lit and calm, decorated with quilts and samplers.

Dena rolled her eyes. "This is how hospitals try to make you think that you're in a friendly, happy place. You should see the delivery room, right through that door." She pointed at the door opposite her bed. "It's high-tech and sterile, like a hospital ought to be. Have you talked to Dr. Mujedin?"

"No. I wanted to see you first. Has he been in?"

"No. Find him, will you?" Dena's legs shifted restlessly under the sheet covering her. She gasped when a contraction hit.

"Breathe, honey, breathe." He grabbed her hand. "Come on, sweetie. You can get through this."

"I know." She puffed. "I've done it before."

"Hey, watch this monitor." Alex pointed at a dark panel with a lime-green squiggle moving across it. As he observed it, the squiggle flattened.

Dena appeared to relax. "That must be the thing strapped to my stomach. It's tracking the contractions.

Let me know when it starts up again, so I have some warning.''

He turned it so she could see the readout. ''I'll get the doctor now.''

Alex left to track down Dr. Mujedin. ''She's impatient and tired,'' he reported.

The doctor raised a dark brow. ''I hope not too tired. This could be a long day for Ms. Randolph.''

''She thinks the baby is going to come fast.''

''That may be.'' The doctor paced down the hall toward Dena's room, Alex by his side.

Dr. Mujedin tapped on Dena's door as she screamed. He ignored her shriek. ''How are we, Ms. Randolph?'' He reached for the chart at the foot of the bed. ''Hmm, six centimeters at nine o'clock. Perhaps we should check this again. Excuse us, Mr. Chandler.''

Alex stepped out while Dr. Mujedin performed the examination. The doctor burst from the room. ''Mr. Chandler, if you want to see this baby born, go down the hall and tell the nurse there to help you scrub up.''

Alex grabbed the doctor's white coat. ''Is it time?''

Dr. Mujedin stopped and smiled. ''Yes, it is. Ms. Randolph is right. This baby is ready to join us.'' He disappeared into Dena's room.

Alex did as he was told. After he'd scrubbed thoroughly and donned sterile garb, a nurse led him into the delivery room. Several hospital personnel, gowned and masked, fluttered around the high-tech chamber. In the center of it all, Dena, covered by a sheet, lay with her legs spread wide. She seemed much calmer, smiling when she saw him.

''Alex.'' She reached for his gloved hand.

''Are you all right?'' He squeezed her fingers gently.

''Dandy, now that the epidural is kicking in.''

He raised his brows. "Good." He stroked strands of red hair, sticky with sweat, away from her face.

Dena panted, body tense with the strain of bearing his child. Images of Dena flowed through Alex's mind as she struggled through labor. Dena, strong and beautiful, digging in the garden. Dena, gentle and caring, wiping a child's tears. Dena, attending Blanche's wedding even though the reminders of Steve must have ripped her heart out.

Dena, giving of herself to everyone she met.

He'd never loved anyone more than at this moment. His heart twisted in his chest as he tried to breathe.

He couldn't bear it if he lost Dena. He had to find a way to make her his. She'd become so much a part of his life, as necessary as his breath.

He loved her. Oh, God, why had it taken him so long to realize how he felt?

He couldn't lose her now. No sacrifice was too great. But what could he do?

He started to speak. "Dena, I lo—"

Dr. Mujedin entered, gloved and masked. Another gowned figure was by his side. "This is Dr. Zeto, a neonatologist."

"Ms. Randolph, Mr. Chandler, there is nothing to fear," Dr. Zeto said. "At this stage, preemies have a survival rate of well over ninety-five percent. Chances are your son or daughter will do fine."

"Much depends upon the next few minutes," Dr. Mujedin said. He glanced down at Dena. "Now, let's get this baby born."

The doctors walked to the end of the table and Dr. Mujedin looked up at a monitor, similar to the one that Alex had seen earlier in Dena's birthing room. As Alex watched, the green line, which had been relatively flat, began to squiggle.

"Now, Ms. Randolph. Push!"

Dena took a deep breath. Alex could see by the focused expression on her face that she knew that *this* was the moment.

"Breathe, honey." Alex stroked her sweaty forehead. "Breathe!"

"He's crowning," Dr. Mujedin said.

"Hang in there, hon, you're doin' great." Alex raced to the foot of Dena's bed.

Dr. Mujedin reached between Dena's legs. "Bear with me, Ms. Randolph. I'm going to give you a little snip—"

Wincing, Alex looked away. Dark spots swam before his vision. He sucked in a deep, desperate breath.

"Push one more time." Dr. Mujedin again reached between Dena's legs. "Come on, now, little one."

Alex started. "What—what are you doing?"

"Just giving your baby a little turn. Shoulders are stuck."

"Is that all?" His baby was in high-tech heaven, but the doctor did nothing more elaborate than slip his fingers into Dena to help the baby out.

"My baby! That's my baby!" Dena screamed, reaching for the infant.

Mujedin looked at Alex. Above the mask, the doctor's solemn, dark eyes seemed a little damp. "You have a beautiful baby daughter, Mr. Chandler." He tenderly placed the baby on Dena's belly.

Alex stared, fascinated and more than a little overwhelmed. Nothing he'd read or studied had prepared him for this moment.

She was so tiny, so fragile, and yet so lovely, his

spindly, wrinkled elf curled on Dena's stomach. He touched one of her fleshy, wedge-shaped feet with a tentative finger, seized with a mad desire to kiss the tender sole of his baby's foot, nuzzle each charming little toe.

"Oh, my God, Alex..." Dena touched the top of his daughter's head with a hesitant finger. "She's perfect."

"And so are you." Alex kissed her forehead. "You're wonderful, honey, and I love you so much."

Reaching up, she twined an arm around his neck. "I love you, too, Alex. So much."

"Mr. Chandler, would you like to cut the cord?" Dr. Zeto brandished a shiny pair of scissors.

All the air whooshed out of Alex's lungs. He reached for the instrument with a trembling hand.

"Right about there, Mr. Chandler." Dr. Mujedin pointed.

Alex snipped. Dizzy, he swayed and clutched the table for support. Oh, God, was he going to faint? He steeled his resolve, biting his lip, willing away the dark spots that again shadowed his vision. He wouldn't let Dena down in this last, ultimate moment, no matter what.

"Very nice." Dr. Mujedin took the scissors from Alex. "Now, let's take these away from you before you hurt yourself. Would you like to sit down?" The doctor sounded amused.

Alex sat while Dr. Zeto and a nurse wrapped his daughter in a towel and took her to a warmer. Dr. Mujedin bent over Dena, encouraging her to push out the placenta before he stitched her up. Alex dropped his head between his knees and groaned, glad he hadn't eaten breakfast.

At last able to relax, Dena looked over at Alex. She couldn't help grinning at the sight. He looked as though he was about to toss his cookies all over the delivery room.

But he hadn't left her. Realization flashed over all of Dena's synapses, like a meteor blazing across the sky.

Alex hadn't left her, even though he'd almost passed out from stress.

Alex would never leave her.

She had to tell him that, finally, she knew. "Uh, Alex—"

Dr. Zeto broke in. "Okay. She's six pounds even and nineteen inches long. Blood pressure, pulse and respiration within normal limits."

Alex staggered to his feet, then over to Dena's side. Now the nurses were helping her out of the soiled gown, then onto a gurney. An orderly draped a fresh sheet over Dena, covering her to the shoulders.

He kissed her flushed cheek. "I love you, honey."

"I love you, too." Dena framed his face with her hands. "Oh, Alex, thank you so very much. I wouldn't have missed this for anything in the world." Tears of happiness spilled down her cheeks.

He kissed them away, his own eyes flooding. Strangely, that seemed to make her cry harder. "Honey, stop, you'll hurt yourself."

She took a couple of gulping breaths. "I c-can't help it. I love you and the baby so much that I—I—" She buried her face in his shoulder.

"I know. I know." He hugged her tight, then released her to kiss her sweet face over and over again. He never wanted to finish loving her.

Dr. Zeto cleared his throat. "Excuse me. We'd like to move mother and baby to a room."

Alex stepped aside to allow the doctor to place his daughter in Dena's arms. She dropped the sheet, then moved the baby's mouth against her breast. After a few hesitant moments, when the infant didn't seem to know what to do, her tiny, budlike mouth opened and sucked on Dena's nipple.

With a faraway calmness in her eyes, Dena tucked the baby more securely into the crook of her arm and leaned back against the pillows. *A natural,* Alex realized. He bet that this was why Tamara had picked her half sister. Dena had an inborn talent for mothering.

Alex's heart swelled with so much love he thought it would split wide open. "So...should we name the baby after Tamara?"

An orderly began to push the gurney out of the delivery room. Alex kept his hand on Dena's shoulder as they walked.

Dena blinked and seemed to reenter normal reality, but didn't meet his gaze. "Alex, this isn't my baby, remember?" She choked slightly, then whispered, "You—you don't need my permission to do anything. I'm not her mother." She murmured the words as though her heart were breaking.

"Aw, honey." He gave his voice a low, reassuring pitch. "I meant what I said back in the delivery room. I love you. And you're all the mother that this baby will ever need. Darling, will you marry me? Please?"

She drew in a breath. Her chest heaved. She looked up at him, eyes wide and questioning. "But—but what about T-Tamara?"

He waited to answer until the orderly turned the gurney, then wheeled it into a room with two empty beds. Dena thrust baby Tami at Alex.

Accepting the tiny, blanketed bundle, Alex gasped with surprise. She was so light, like dandelion fluff in his hands. Captivated, he stared at her little, reddish face.

She had dark-blue eyes in a shade he'd never before seen, surmounted by a skimpy halo of pale golden hair. "She's gorgeous," he murmured.

Her pouty mouth opened, showing him adorable, toothless gums. She emitted a plaintive cry.

The orderly helped Dena onto a freshly made bed before he left.

"She's still hungry, I bet." Dena eased back against the pillows with a happy-sounding sigh. She reached for the baby.

He carefully nestled her back into Dena's arms. Baby Tami flailed her wee, soft hands, searching for her mother's nipple. Dena guided the infant to her other breast. The baby settled into her snack.

"I don't mean to be impatient, but are you going to say yes, or not?"

"Alex—" Dena took a deep, shuddering breath. "We have some things we have to talk about. You were my half sister's husband. I can't help feeling that I'm betraying her somehow."

His heart sank. If she really felt that way, there was no hope. But he didn't believe her. She'd just told him that she loved him. They'd come close to making love more than once. *Perhaps she's just playing devil's advocate,* he thought.

"I'll always love and honor Tamara's memory. And my love for her isn't lessened by loving you. I still think about her often, most often when I'm with you."

She looked surprised. "Most people don't think she was much like me."

"They're wrong." He caressed her face. "Your sense of humor and your honesty are just like hers. But it doesn't make me sad. Because of you, I can remember Tamara with joy. I have to go on, Dena. She would have wanted me to. And I love you more than I dreamed possible." Alex squeezed Dena's free hand.

"Are you sure you're not marrying me because of the baby?" Dena's eyes were wide and serious.

"Absolutely." He sat on the bed beside her. "Or, as you'd put it, 'Sure, I'm sure.'" His teasing grin failed to elicit her smile.

"Truly, Alex, I have to know."

He took her free hand in both of his. "Dena, I'd never do that. You're my life and my heart and everything that makes me happy. I want you because I love you, because you complete my life in a way I need and want and must have."

"But Alex, this has been a very emotional day. I can't be the same kind of wife that Tamara was. I'm really not like her."

"You're like…you. I love you, Dena, I really do. Don't you believe me?"

She looked at him, her eyes misty. "I'd like to. I love you so much that I know I can't possibly live without you. But I learned the hard way that sometimes love…just isn't enough."

"Steve really burned you, didn't he?"

"Yeah, he did. I thought I was really in love and it would last forever." A rueful smile flitted over her face. "After losing him, I couldn't trust my judgment anymore."

He squeezed her hand. "Then trust mine. We're perfect for each other."

"How can you be so sure?"

He hesitated before withdrawing his pad from his pocket. He sat down on the side of her bed, then flipped to the pro-con page.

"Oh, my God, Alex. You made a *list?*" Dena threw

back her head and roared with laughter. She laughed so hard that tears leaked from the corners of her eyes.

The baby looked up and drooled, which set Dena off again. She grabbed a tissue from a box next to the bed and dabbed at her eyes. "Oh, Alex. Sweet, compulsive, neurotic Alex. What can I do with you?"

"Marry me." He waved the pad in the air. "Here's why." He thrust the list at her, holding it so she could read without shifting the baby.

Her eyes widened. "'Sex goddess?' 'Reasonably attractive?' I'm a reasonably attractive sex goddess?" She started to laugh some more. "Oh, Alex, I do love you so much. 'A good parent.'" She looked up at him. "Just remember that when we argue about the children."

"Then you'll say yes?" He dropped the pad onto the sheet beside her.

Her eyes overflowed with tears. "Oh, yes, Alex. Yes, yes, yes!" She reached out for him with her free hand, lacing her fingers between his.

He lifted her hand to kiss it, feeling both humbled and proud. Although babies were born every day, few men and women accomplished the miracle of love. "I'm a lucky man," he said aloud. "I've loved, and been loved by two extraordinary women."

Dena blushed. "Thank you," she whispered. "I'm very grateful for you. I never thought this could happen to me."

Alex sat on the bed beside her and wrapped an arm around her shoulders. They cuddled together quietly, watching their daughter nurse.

The gap that had been torn in his heart when Tamara died had healed, leaving him complete and whole. Miraculously, her illness and death hadn't left a scar. He wondered why, then realized that loving Dena and the twins helped fill the terrible chasm in his life. Now he could recall Tamara with delight, not sorrow.

He chuckled. ''I can't help remembering what your mom said about Tami.''

''What?''

''Irina said at Greg's wedding that she thought that Tamara had manipulated us all into this situation.''

''I bet Mom's right.'' Dena looked heavenward and smiled. ''Thank you, Tami.'' She shifted her gaze to Alex. ''Yeah, let's name the baby after Tamara. She'd have liked that. Now, let's check out the rest of this list. What did you put on the 'con' side?''

He snatched it away. ''Uh, you don't need to read this right now. Or ever.''

''If I weren't stuck in this bed, I'd get it from you.'' She narrowed her green eyes at him.

He tore the page out of the pad and ripped it into tiny pieces, then kicked them under the bed. ''All gone, along with any doubts.'' Leaning over her, he kissed her again, then whispered, ''I love you more and more each day.''

The baby stopped suckling, so Dena rang for a nurse to take the baby. Dena nestled back against the pillows with a sense of contentment that she never thought she'd achieve. She'd loved Steve with the impetuosity of youth, the way a restless girl wants the excitement of the unknown. She'd never before understood the devotion that true love entailed.

Alex had shown her what love meant. She now had a mature love, the love of her life, the man who'd be by her side forever.

Epilogue

When all the wedding guests had left and they'd put the kids to bed, Alex took his wife's hand and led her to their bedroom to begin their honeymoon. He'd anticipated this night for months. He and baby Tami had stayed at Dena's since the baby's birth, but he hadn't wanted the twins to see them as lovers before marriage. Dena also thought intimacy would send the wrong message, so he'd slept in baby Tami's room. Today he'd moved into the bedroom he'd share with his wife.

"Something in me wants everyone to have what we've got," Alex told his wife. He kicked off his shoes and shrugged out of his jacket.

"You're a sweetheart, but our kind of love is a rare thing." The brightness in Dena's eyes dimmed.

He guessed she was thinking of Steve. "Don't," he said. "Not tonight." He reached around her and slid her zipper down.

Her smile reappeared. "Okay." She let the dress drop to the floor, then stepped over the circle of ivory silk, kicking off her shoes. Clad only in a white, strapless teddy and stockings, she walked to her dresser with a seductive wriggle of her hips.

Turning her head, she winked at him over one shapely shoulder. "It's a deal." Dena withdrew a sheaf of papers from her dresser drawer. "Speaking of deals, what happens to this one?" With a sassy grin, she waved the papers in front of her breasts, temptingly framed by the white lace of the sexy lingerie.

He looked at the surrogacy contract. His face flamed. "Oh, that."

Dena gave him a big, wicked smile. "Yeah, that." Flipping it open, she read, "The party of the second part agrees to terminate all parental rights to the aforementioned baby."

He grabbed for the document, but she evaded him. Giggling, she danced around their bed. "Contact between the aforementioned baby and the party of the second part shall be limited to activities approved by the party of the first part."

"Give me that!" He'd shred every one of the embarrassing pages into a million pieces. How could he have been such a jerk?

"The party of the first part shall control—and that's what it's about, huh, Alex, control—" She let out a full-throated guffaw.

"Quiet. You'll wake the kids." Jumping across the bed, he snatched the contract from her hand and ripped it across the middle. He flung the scraps over his shoulder.

"Darn," she said. "I thought I could tease you with

that forever. I should make you eat those words, Alex Chandler.''

He smiled. ''Yes, you could.''

''But I'm a kind, gentle, forgiving woman.''

''Oh, baby, are you ever.'' He reached for her, taking her face in both hands.

''And I love you.'' Her kiss was a sultry, sexy promise of bliss.

He kissed her back, his heart overflowing with happiness. ''Me, too. I'm yours, baby, every minute of every day.'' He wiggled his fingers beneath the lacy edge of the teddy.

Dena giggled.

He stopped, a comical, chastened expression on his face. ''What's funny?''

''Your wiggly fingers.''

''Huh?''

''You know, life has such strange twists and turns. I once thought I'd never want to make love to you, that I'd rather snuggle with a sea snake.''

''A sea snake? Where did that come from?''

''Wiggly fingers…and you seemed so cold and detached.'' Leaning forward, she looped one arm around his neck and began to unbutton his shirt with the other. ''But now—''

''I'm just not a show-off.''

''Smug, aren't we?'' She slipped her hand inside his shirt and caressed him until his eyes darkened to midnight blue.

''I have a lot to be smug about.'' He nuzzled her ear, his lips soft and warm against the lobe. ''You, for example.''

A rustle from the baby monitor alerted him. Dena's

head also turned. A tiny, piping voice issued from the speaker. "Be real quiet, Miri."

"I am." Another rustle. "Isn't she *cute?*" Miri's voice rose to a squeak.

Alex caught Dena's gaze and they exchanged smiles. The twins had grown to adore their baby sister, vying for her attention.

"We'd better get in there before they wake her up," Dena whispered. Donning her robe, she crept out of their room and down the hall. Alex followed.

Now, just outside the baby's room, he could hear Jack. "Do you think she'd miss her Paddington Bear?"

"Hey!" Alex stage-whispered. "What are you two doing up?"

Two dark heads jerked, swiveling around to regard him with identical expressions of mock innocence.

"We was just checking on the baby." Jack's eyes were round and guileless.

"Were," Alex said.

"Were what?" Miriam asked.

"You two *were* checking on Tami."

"Yeah," the twins chorused.

Tami blinked, yawned and stretched, reaching for Alex.

"You woke her up, Jack." Miriam glared at her brother.

Alex picked up the baby and cuddled her close, sniffing the delightful scents of clean daughter and talcum powder. "Come to Daddy, sweetheart." He'd never tire of snuggling with his precious daughter. He loved her more than his life.

Tami scrabbled at the opening of his shirt.

He grinned. "I think she wants you, honey." After kissing her forehead, he handed the baby to Dena.

She sat in the rocker, discreetly opened just the top of her robe, and tugged down her lingerie so she could feed Tami.

"I don't get it, Uncle Alex," Jack said. "You're married to my mom. You're my sister's dad. How come you're not my dad, too?"

His heart pounding triple-time, Alex sought and captured Dena's gaze. They'd waited for months for the twins to ask this question, discussing this topic at least, well, ten thousand times.

Despite numerous explanations to the twins about surrogate mothers, the kids persisted in believing the baby was Dena's...and, in a sense, they were right. Baby Tami had two mothers, one biological and absent, one present and very much alive.

Dena audibly sucked in a deep breath, shifting the baby at her breast. "He can be your daddy, for real, if you both want him to be." Anyone else would hear only a casual tone of voice, but he and Dena had become very close. Alex could hear a slight edge of anxiety rimming her words.

"What about Other Daddy, the one in 'Rabia?" Miriam demanded. Steve occasionally called, or sent cash and gifts. The twins knew of him, though they'd never met. He resided in Riyadh, enjoying the lush life of an oil industry executive. When Alex and Dena had phoned to talk with Steve about the possibility of Alex adopting the twins, Steve had been blasé about the issue.

"It's okay with Other Daddy," Dena said.

Alex saw Miri and Jack look at each other, sharing a moment of the special communication the twins shared. "Okay," they chorused.

The tension swept out of Alex, leaving his muscles limp and drained. "Thanks, kids," he managed to say.

Miriam grabbed his hand. "Does that mean we're supposed to call you Daddy now?" She swung his arm back and forth.

"Or do we have to go to the courthouse, like on TV?" Jack asked, pressing his small body up against Alex, as though searching for a hug.

Alex wrapped his arm around Jack's shoulders, his heart too full for words.

"Don't worry about the paperwork, Jack. You can call him Daddy now." Dena transferred Tami to her other breast.

"Dad-dee! Dad-dee!" Miriam capered around the room.

Tami released Dena's nipple and burped loudly. The twins exploded with laughter.

"All right, gang, it's bedtime." Dena stood, putting Tami up to her shoulder. The baby responded with another noisy belch.

Jack burped right back.

Everyone whooped, including baby Tami, who opened her toothless mouth in a big, gummy smile.

Later, back in their room, Dena lay back on the pillows, her soul replete with a fulfillment she hadn't known she could reach. He was here, and he was hers. Alex, her lover and husband, the father of all her children, always and forever.

He massaged the ball of her right foot, sending tingles of pleasure throughout the sole.

"Bless you, my darling." She closed her eyes, in total bliss. Was she the luckiest woman in the world?

He chuckled, then rubbed her baby toe. "This little piggy went to market..."

She giggled. She had a good idea of where "all the way home" was.

"This little piggy stayed home." He nibbled at her second toe, making her squeal.

"This little piggy had roast beef." Alex moved on, squeezing her middle toe. She sighed with delight.

"This little piggy had none. And this little piggy…" He looked up, his eyes alight with mischief. "Said wee-wee-wee-wee all the way home." He tickled up her calf to her inner thigh.

Hot desire cascaded through every cell as Alex's clever, knowing touch incited her passion. "I'm a lucky woman."

"And I'm a lucky guy."

In unison, they looked heavenward and said, "Thank you, Tami."

And laughed with joy.

*   *   *   *   *

Author's notes and Acknowledgments

I have taken numerous liberties with the in vitro fertilization procedure mentioned in this book. Don't rely upon this novel for medical advice or even for information about the complex IVF method. My critique partners, Cheryl Clark, Caroline Cummings, Judy Dedek, Jackie Hamilton, Sylvia Renfro and Jane Shirah, were enormously helpful in polishing this novel. Writer Tina Hilmas, a neonatal nurse, gave me advice with the last two chapters. My editor, Kim Nadelson, patiently shepherded me through the publication process. Thank you, Kim!

As always, I owe my deepest thanks to my husband, who nurtures and supports me in every possible way.

Modern Romance™
...seduction and
passion guaranteed

Tender Romance™
...love affairs that
last a lifetime

Medical Romance™
...medical drama
on the pulse

Historical Romance™
...rich, vivid and
passionate

Sensual Romance™
...sassy, sexy and
seductive

Blaze Romance™
...the temperature's
rising

27 new titles every month.

Live the emotion

MILLS & BOON®

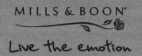

MILLS & BOON®

BETTY NEELS

THE CHRISTMAS COLLECTION

On sale 5th December 2003

*Available at most branches of WH Smith, Tesco, Martins, Borders,
Eason, Sainsbury's and all good paperback bookshops.*

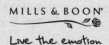

MILLS & BOON®

Live the emotion

PENNINGTON

Catherine George
PENNINGTON
Leader of the Pack

MILLS & BOON

BOOK SIX

Available from 5th December 2003

*Available at most branches of WHSmith, Tesco, Martins, Borders,
Eason, Sainsbury's and most good paperback bookshops.*

PENN/RTL/6